UNIVERSES

Kendra H. Slee

A Love to Last

© 2021 **Europe Books**| London
www.europebooks.co.uk | info@europebooks.co.uk

ISBN 979-12-201-1381-6

First edition: November 2021
Distribution for the United Kingdom: **Vine House Distribution ltd**

Printed for Italy by *Rotomail Italia S.p.A. - Vignate (MI)*
Stampato presso *Rotomail Italia S.p.A. - Vignate (MI)*

A Love to Last

Chapter One

When Madison pulled her Volkswagen into the maintenance shop's parking lot at Middleton Golf Club, she was surprised to see a beat-up, black, pick-up truck already there.

Throughout her nearly ten years of working maintenance at a golf course, she had always made sure she woke early enough to enjoy a few moments of the mornings' noises and calmness. When she lived in Mississauga, she was usually one of the only cars on the road as she made her way to Ruby Lewis Golf & Country Club, and that was a reprieve from the city's regular hustle and bustle.

Here in Meaford, though, there was silence everywhere. As she drove to work, she felt like she was the only person in the entire town. Traffic lights changed for no one, each road bare except for nocturnal animals scampering across, lamp posts remained lit for no one, and, if it weren't for the cars parked in driveways, homes would have looked vacant.

Madison parked next to the truck and took a deep breath. Aside from the whirlwind past two months she had had, starting a new job in a new town was not helping her nerves. But it was what she needed.

It wasn't the job itself that was making her anxious because Madison had started working groundskeeping when she was fifteen year old. She had begun with just watering flowers, pulling weeds, raking bunkers, and doing other menial tasks, but she took great pride in her work making sure the flower beds and sand traps looked pristine each day. It didn't take Madison long to recognize that she was working in a male-dominated industry, and to be considered an equal, she would have to work harder than her colleagues. She began staying later and arriving to work earlier than everyone else and when her superintendent,

Evan, finally asked her why, she replied, 'If you're early, you're on time; if you're on time, you're late; and if you're late, that's unacceptable.'

Evan quickly began giving Madison other jobs that required a bit more training, and when she turned sixteen and got her G1 driver's license, she was trained on the *Sandpro*, the *Sidewinder*, and on the *Groundsmaster* rough mowers. By the end of her first summer, she also learned how to cut fairways, tees, approaches, and greens. It took the rest of the crew some time to come around to the idea of a teenage girl working with them, but her hard work and dedication earned her respect amongst them. She was encouraged to return the following year, and, what was once supposed to be a summer job started to become a possible second career option for her.

After eight seasons at Ruby Lewis, and with Madison's responsibilities growing each year, Evan offered her a second assistant's position upon her graduation from Ryerson University for journalism *if* she took the proper golf management courses at the University of Guelph the following fall.

Madison had initially accepted the offer on the condition that it would not be permanent because she eventually wanted to write for a newspaper. However, in the meantime while working at Ruby Lewis she could be a freelance writer so she could build her portfolio and, by having a career at the golf course, Madison would be able to support herself as she did that. But then everything came to a life-altering stop and the world as she knew it flipped upside down; everything she had once thought to be important ceased to matter. Madison found it difficult to cope in her normal environment and needed to escape.

Lights inside the maintenance building turned on, just as Madison completed doing some breathing exercises in her car. The building was a 'T' shape and she was surprised by how much newer and larger it looked in person compared to the photos she viewed online.

Directly in front of her car was the long vertical part of the shop that she could guess stored the machinery and tools. To its immediate right and diagonally from her, there were large windows and a side door which she assumed was where the offices, bathrooms and lunchroom were; meaning that the other end of the building was the mechanic's bay.

Madison checked her cell phone for the time and took one final deep breath before she got out of her car.

As she walked towards the building's side entrance, other vehicles began to pull in. As each car drove by, its passengers nodded 'hello' to her and she nodded back.

Just as she had almost made it to the side door, a jeep with 'Go Topless!!' sprawled across its windshield came ripping into the parking lot.

You've got to be kidding me, she thought, turning to open the door to the building. But it was too late, the door had opened on her.

"ARGH!" she cried. Madison had been standing at the right angle for her head to take the brunt of the collision. Holding her face in her hands, she keeled over.

"Oh, no!" a man shouted. "Are you okay?"

"What do you think?" she fumed.

"I'm sorry, I was walking backwards out the door, like an idiot, and didn't see you."

Madison could see through her fingers that the man had bent over and was trying to see if she were okay. She felt a hand on her shoulder. "Don't touch me!" she hissed.

"Sorry!" he said quickly backing away.

Madison slowly stood upright and removed her hands from her face, examining them for blood.

"Oh, that doesn't look good." She heard the man say.

She refocused her eyes on him and her chest clenched. He was a few inches taller than her and wore a black golf shirt tucked into brown work pants. He had blonde hair under a baseball cap, some scruff on his face, and piercingly blue eyes that screamed remorse, and Madison immediately regretted how short she had been. He was broad shouldered, and, from the fit of his shirt, it was easy to tell he took care of himself.

"Your lip's bleeding," he said snapping Madison out of her daze. "We should get some ice on it to try and halt the swelling." He turned back towards the door and opened it, but Madison took a step backwards raising her eyebrows.

He lifted his hands in a helpless gesture. "I'm an 'accidentally open a door on a lady one time' kind of guy."

"Alright, but I do have a retaliation quota...." she replied walking past him.

"That's fair. There are a couple bathrooms inside but use the second one on the left down the hall, it's the one Jules uses, so, it's cleaner. There's also a first aid kit in there."

When Madison walked into the building, she saw that there were two offices across from each other and the hallway was covered in photographs of the construction stages of the golf course. The hallway opened into a medium sized lunchroom equipped with two fridges, a microwave, a couple of coffee makers, a dishwasher, a bookshelf full of what looked like user manuals for their machines, and a massive chalkboard listing everyone's name and their jobs for the day. Diagonally from where she stood there was a door with a sign that said 'Shop' above it and, directly in front of her, another room with lockers lined along its side.

"It's just in there," he said pointing to the bathroom while he walked towards the freezer.

Madison entered the single stall bathroom and was astonished when she saw her reflection in the mirror. The left side of her face had a thick red line down it from where the door had connected, and her lips had a streak of blood across them. "Wow, you really know how to welcome new employees," she said dryly.

"I'm really sorry. Madison, right? I'm Jake Andrews," he said sticking out his hand as he entered the bathroom. He pulled some paper towel from the dispenser and wrapped it around the ice he had in his other hand.

They stood staring at each other for several moments until they heard one of the shop door's open and someone yell.

"Oh, Jaaakkkeee!"

He sighed and handed her the ice. "In a completely non-threatening way, do you mind if I close the door?"

Madison's eyebrows furrowed. "Sure?"

Once closed, he pushed the button on its knob to lock it. "Still in a completely non-threatening way, I'm just locking it, so you're spared a few more minutes from meeting Robbie. Think of the most annoying seventeen-year-old boy from high school, and, I mean this in a loving way, times that by a hundred and that's Robbie. But he's harmless."

"Come on, Jakey!" Robbie yelled again right outside the door this time.

"Let me guess, he's the one that drives the 'Go Topless' jeep?" Madison asked.

"Bingo."

"Charming."

"He's actually a good kid, just very immature." Jake coughed and spoke louder through the door, "Put the coffee on, Robbie," he mouthed 'sorry' as he moved around Madison and unlocked the first aid kit. He took out a couple of antiseptic pads, polysporin, and band-aids. He handed Madison the antiseptic pads, and she began lightly rubbing her cheeks, wincing as she rubbed them over her lips.

"I'm sorry, again."

"You've said that, like four times, already."

"I know but saying it just once doesn't make it alright."

Madison was stunned by his words and surprised by how nonchalantly he had said it. If only more people believed that and meant it, she thought.

"If you're okay in here, I should continue writing everyone's jobs on the chalkboard."

"Are you the assistant superintendent here?" she asked uncertainly.

"Sort of, but not really. Just unofficially, officially in charge when Drew isn't here. Drew was super impressed with your resume, so he wants to start you on greens. I'll go with you this morning, we'll cut together, and leapfrog with Robbie and Oskar." He grabbed the door handle but paused. "So, you're okay in here?"

Madison nodded, and Jake slipped out of the bathroom. Once she was alone, she took a deep breath while placing the ice back on her lips. The band-aids were only large sized, so she decided against putting them on. By the time the swelling had gone down enough, and she opened the bathroom door, everyone else had left to start their jobs. Jake stood at the chalkboard writing peoples' second and third tasks for the day on it, and Madison couldn't help but think how efficient Middleton Golf Club seemed already.

In the top right corner of the chalkboard, Madison read, 'Welcome Madison! We'll chat at lunch!'

"Who wrote that?" she asked pointing.

"Jules. She's super pumped to have another woman on staff." He put the chalk down and turned around. "If you could put mine, Drew's and Scott's phone numbers into your cell and then text us your name so that we know that that's your number, that'd be great. Scott's also unofficially, officially in charge here with me when Drew is away. We don't use walkie-talkies, so we communicate through text or phone calls. If there are any important messages, we'll write them here on the chalkboard but also text them to you. Feel free to call or text us while you're out on the golf course with any questions you might have. If you brought a lunch you could put it in one of the fridges, and any extra gear, your purse, keys or whatever you can put in your locker just in there. I think the first one as soon as you walk into the locker room is empty."

"Thanks, but I can get all of that stuff from my car later."

He smiled. "Follow me then."

Jake walked through the locker room and opened another door that way kitty-corner to the lunchroom. Entering the drive shed, it was practically now bare from all of the machinery and tools because the other workers had already left with them, but it was evident to Madison that everything in the drive shed was organized and had its proper place. As she walked through, she saw that all the shelves or things hanging from hooks were labeled. Leaf, shrub, and bunker rakes were hanging neatly marked, as were shovels with clear tags for flat, spade, and snow removal. The shed floor was swept clean, and none of the shelves she passed had even a layer of dust or dirt on them. Not that Ruby Lewis's maintenance building was a pigsty, Madison made sure of that, but out of all the other golf courses she had visited none of them had shops as clean as this one.

As if reading her mind, Jake said, "If you're wondering why it's so clean, Scott runs a tight ship."

"Is he responsible for the flowers in the bathroom and lunchroom, too?"

"Jules runs a tight ship in there," he said smirking.

Madison was impressed. "This is the most organized and clean maintenance building that I have ever been in!"

Jake laughed. "Please don't tell Scott or Jules that, they don't need anyone else tooting their horns about how clean and organized they are."

"Well, most maintenance shops I've been in are disasters with dirt and grass everywhere, machines parked in an un-Tetris fashion, and no one putting anything back where they're supposed to so then everyone wastes so much time in the morning trying to find what they need." Madison stopped walking and stared in front of her. "Is that golf cart and trailer with walkers on it already set-up for us?" she asked in disbelief.

He laughed. "Yeah, I did that this morning. It's kind of my thing. I get here before everyone else, set everything up for the jobs of the day so when people arrive, they don't waste time finding things."

Madison made a mental note that if she were ever to continue her career in golf course maintenance that she would do something similar. She couldn't help but wonder why she hadn't thought of that herself. "Smart."

"You've worked maintenance at a golf course for a long time, right? How'd you get into it?" Jake asked as they got into their golf cart. When he saw her look uncomfortable, he quickly added, "I only ask because Jules is the only other woman, I've ever met to have worked at a golf course as long as you. Which is a shame, but that's why I'm curious."

Avoiding answering his question, she inquired, "How did Jules get into it?"

"Because I worked here and helped get her the job. Same with Scott."

"Have you all worked here since Middleton opened?"

"Pretty much," he answered driving them away from the shop and towards the first green they were to cut.

"Why did you start working here?"

"Because working outside with my hands is better than working inside with them."

I couldn't agree more, she thought. From the moment Madison began working at Ruby Lewis she had always found such gratification from seeing the finished product of her hard-physical work, whether it was weeding flower beds, aerating grass, laying sod, tree trimming or cutting grass, she always felt satisfied at the end of each day.

"And, of course, the free golf," he continued. "Do you play?"

"Not really," she lied. Madison wasn't in Meaford to make friends, so she didn't want anyone knowing too much about her and admitting she played golf would lead to invitations to play that she didn't want to accept. Not to mention that there were things she didn't want to talk about and knew if she started to open up, conversations would lead where she didn't want them to go.

"That's too bad. Jules was hoping you would. She's tired of golfing with guys all the time."

As they continued to drive along the cart paths to their first green, Madison sensed that Jake wanted to talk more, but was glad that he didn't so she could enjoy and observe her new surroundings in silence.

They passed Robbie cutting the putting greens and Oskar on the first hole, so Madison inferred that they would start on the second green. As they drove closer, she could see that it was sandwiched between two bunkers and had a little pond to the right of it before the approach started.

"Did you use walker mowers at Ruby Lewis?" Jake asked getting out of their golf cart and walking towards the trailer. He unhinged the back and unlocked the driver's side wheel locks while Madison did the same on her side.

"Yeah, my last four years there we switched from triplex mowers to them."

"Great. How comfortable do you feel operating walkers?"

To anyone who knew the extent of Madison's experience at Ruby Lewis, Jake's question would seem irrelevant, but she had made sure that her resume didn't reveal her true level of experience and she asked Evan, her old Superintendent, not to mention it either. This meant that neither Drew, Jake or Scott knew that Madison had read all their machines' user manuals and could recite how they work and how to fix them word for word.

"Fairly comfortable," she responded, pulling the first walker off the trailer. "What's the cutting schedule for today?"

"There's a cutting chart sticker on the inside of the walker's handle, but today is four to ten with no clean-up. I'll start fixing ball marks and take the pin out if you want to make the first cut?"

Madison nodded, switched her walker on and pulled its start cord. Using the middle of the approach as six o'clock, Madison walked to where four o'clock would be and picked a tree on the other side of the green to stare at. Once she turned the cutting reels on and began walking, she kept her eyes focused on the tree despite feeling Jake's eyes watching her. When she finished the first pass, Madison knew her line was perfectly straight and didn't hesitate on her turn to double check before starting the second pass.

When she finished cutting her side of the green, she walked her mower back to their golf cart and loaded it on the trailer. After locking its wheels in, Jake followed behind her with his walker and locked it in place, too.

"Impressive lines!"

"Thanks."

"So where is Ruby Lewis Golf & Country Club anyways?" he asked, getting into the golf cart and driving them to their next green. "I've heard of it but have no clue where it actually is."

Madison hesitated. "Just outside of Toronto."

"Oh, so you're from Toronto?"

"Give or take," she replied flippantly and could tell he was surprised by her continuously vague answers.

Jake tried a different question. "What brought you to Meaford?"

Madison gave Jake a sympathetic smile. "Let's not talk about me."

"Yeah, sure, no worries. I was just trying to get to know you," he responded casually.

"I know."

They drove to the fifth green silently and while Madison was thankful for it, she couldn't help but feel bad for the awkwardness she had created between them.

Once they arrived at the fifth hole, Jake pulled their cart off the path and parked it in the rough. Leaning forward on its steering wheel, he said, "I didn't think it was supposed to rain today."

"Me either," she replied following his gaze towards ominous looking clouds that were fast approaching.

"Was that your Volkswagen next to my truck? Uh, sorry, forget I-"

Madison now felt even worse for being so standoffish earlier and softly smiled. "Yes, that's Hank, but I think you meant next to your 'beat-up' truck."

Jake looked appalled as he unlocked his walker's wheels and pulled it off the trailer. "That's a 1967 Chevrolet C-10. She's a beauty, thank you very much!"

"1967 was a good year for trucks, I'll give you that, but 1955 was even better. Like a Chevy Cameo Carrier for example." Madison rolled her walker off the trailer and began walking towards the green. "I'll make the first cut, again," she called over her shoulder.

As Madison made another incredible first cut, Jake fixed the ball marks and pulled the pin out. Just as he was about to begin cutting the other half of the green, there was a loud crack of thunder above them. They both jumped. Madison was mid-turn and quickly turned the cutting reels off while setting her mower down. They looked at the threatening clouds above them just as another loud crack sounded. With their mowers still running, and being on opposite ends of the green, it was too loud to hear one another, so Jake stuck his index finger towards the sky and made a small, fast circle signaling they were done for now and heading back in.

"The maintenance shop is close, so we'll head there until the storm passes," he said as they quickly loaded their walkers onto the trailer.

As Jake started to drive them, Madison tried to mentally figure out the layout of Middleton. Based on the research she had done before beginning there, and what she'd already seen from their morning drive, she estimated it would take them three minutes to make it back to the shop before the rain.

However, within seconds it had begun to torrential downpour and the golf cart they were in didn't have a roof.

"ARGH!" they both exclaimed.

"The rain's so cold!" she yelled.

Jake laughed in disbelief. "Wow!"

In a preventative effort, Madison moved forward in her seat so she wouldn't be sitting in a puddle of water.

"I don't think that's going to help much, my pants are already soaked through!"

"This is ridiculous!" she shouted.

Jake took his baseball cap off and shook his head. Madison couldn't help but notice the nice wave of his hair that had been hiding underneath his hat earlier. The surrealness and spontaneity of the moment caught Madison off guard. She cupped her hands to see how fast they would fill with water and within seconds the water was spilling out of them. Forgetting everything, she threw the puddle of water from her hands onto Jake.

"Are you for real?" he shouted, but his smile was unmistakable.

Madison let out a hearty laugh and realized as she was doing it that she hadn't laughed like that in months. "Does Meaford normally get rain like this?" she asked leaning in, so she didn't have to yell so loudly.

Jake mimicked her and leaned in as well before responding. "It hasn't rained like this in years! But if it keeps up our bunkers are going to be flooded!"

"They don't have drainage?"

"Most do, but they weren't installed very well, so they're clogged more often than not."

"Why not fix them then?" she asked passively knowing it was something she had easily done many times at Ruby Lewis.

"Not enough time. Only Drew or I know how to do that. Scott can, but he's not the most confident with it. Plus, it would be too big of a project, and there are too many other things to do!"

Madison looked ahead of them and squinted. "I don't know how you're driving right now; this rain is coming down thick! I can't see a thing!"

"I can't see anything either!" He joked, shaking the steering wheel, making the cart jerk back and forth.

"Are you trying to hit every puddle?" she asked smirking.

"Would it matter?"

They finally reached the maintenance building a few minutes later than she had estimated. Both mechanic doors in the drive shed were still open, so Jake drove their cart through one of them and parked in front of the other one. They sat in silence for a few seconds as they watched the storm continue to wreak its havoc.

"Where's everyone else?" Madison finally asked.

"Probably at the halfway house or the clubhouse waiting for a text from Scott or me. We were just closest to the shop, which is why I brought us here. So, in the future, wherever you're closest to in a thunderstorm, just hang out there until you hear from me, Scott or Drew."

Madison stood up slowly from the golf cart and attempted to pull her sticky clothes off her skin.

"Did you bring extra clothes?" Jake asked.

Madison nodded. "And towels, extra shoes, socks...."

"Wow, you are the most prepared worker I've ever met."

She looked at her sopping wet clothes. "Not exactly. Bringing my rain gear in our cart this morning would have been a smart idea."

"Well, the rain was unexpected. You know, these kinds of storms are pretty awesome, though. Especially when watching them over the lake from the harbour," he said, getting up from the cart. "Excuse me; I'm just going to call Scott and figure out our game plan."

Madison leaned against the garage door frame and stared out at the raging storm while trying to avoid letting her thoughts drift too far; at least not here. When she was back in the comfort of the cottage, that was when she would allow her memories to get the best of her.

"Alright, Scott says the bunkers around the half-way house are full already, and I just looked at the radar and the storm's not letting up anytime soon. I'm going to send everyone a 'Victoria's' text which means we're calling it a day and going out for breakfast as a crew. It's a tradition here on rainy days to go there when the day finishes so early. You up for it?"

Ignoring his question, she asked, "What about washing our walkers or the rest of the greens that haven't been cut?"

"Oh, I'll wash them after the storm breaks and if it's dry enough Scott and I will come back in the afternoon and finish cutting the greens," he answered waving her off. "Quite the first day you're having, eh? How do your lips and face feel?"

"Fine."

"So, what do you think? Will you join us for breakfast? It would be a great way to meet everyone else."

Madison shook her head. "Thank you, but I can't."

Jake looked surprised. "Really?"

"Yeah, I have a lot to do," she lied again. "I arrived late last night, so the unexpected day off will be nice for unpacking.

Thank you, though." Madison smiled before turning around and jogging through the rain to her car before Jake could respond.

Chapter Two

Madison drove along Highway 26 as it followed the shoreline of Georgian Bay. Her windows were down, the sun was shining, and she was smiling as her long brown hair and the warm breeze brushed against her face. Madison felt good, like a weight had been lifted off her shoulders, and it felt like everything was back to normal again. But in an instant the sun and soft breeze were gone, replaced by dark, brooding skies. Lightning and thunder began, and, within seconds, enormous pieces of hail started to fall, cracking the windshield, and denting the hood. She began to panic and tried to do her window up and pull the car off the road, but neither would budge. The pieces of hail were steadily getting bigger and Madison feared they would shatter the windshield. She leaned forward over the steering wheel and saw a massive chunk of hail barreling towards her. She screamed and tried once again to move her car off the road but couldn't. Just as she braced herself for the impact of the humongous piece of hail, the hail turned to snow, and the clouds from black to grey. The wind picked up heavily and was howling through the open windows of her car. Madison tried to roll the driver's side window up again because she had begun to shiver, but it still wouldn't move. She reached across the passenger seat and tried its window only to find it was immovable as well. Madison began to truly panic when something in the rear-view mirror caught her eye.

"Annie!" she practically yelled. "What are you doing here?"

"What do you mean? I live in your car now." Suddenly Annie had moved from the backseat to the passenger seat and was sitting beside her.

"Put your seatbelt on, Annie. I can hardly see in front of me and I'm not able to pull the car over or roll the windows up!"

"What happened to your face?" Annie asked.

Madison touched her lips from where Jake had opened the door. "*I'll tell you about it later, now do your seatbelt up! This isn't funny!"*

"He should have opened the door harder. You deserve worse. I mean, look at me."

"What?" Madison turned to look at her and gasped.

Annie had a gigantic gash on her head that was seeping blood down her face, shattered pieces of glass were lodged into her head and her clothes were torn and blood soaked.

"ANNIE!"

"Have you been drinking?" she asked.

"What? No!" Madison replied hurt, tears welling in her eyes.

"Patrick thinks you have."

Madison scoffed. "*You want to talk about Patrick right now?"*

"Well, it's about time you finally broke up with him. But I agree with him, you must have been drunk when you picked me up…".

"What? How can you say that, Annie? No, I swear -" Madison began before truck headlights crashed into them.

Madison bolted upright in her bed, sweating and panting. It took a few moments for her to collect her bearings before realizing where she was. She looked at the alarm clock on the nightstand, and it flashed 4:17 AM. She buried her face into her hands and took several deep breaths. She knew it would be pointless to try to get back to sleep now, especially when her alarm for work was set to go off shortly, so she kicked off her sheets and made her way to the bathroom.

She squinted against the bathroom light's harsh brightness and examined her lips and face in the mirror. The red line along her cheek had faded surprisingly well and her cut lips were healing nicely too. After brushing her teeth, she applied more ointment to them.

When she changed out of her pajamas and into her work clothes, Madison walked into the kitchen and poured herself a bowl of cereal. Opening the porch door, she sat on the veranda overlooking the moonlit Georgian Bay. Listening to the calmness of the small waves rolling onto shore, helped to relax her.

Madison's thoughts drifted back to her nightmare. They had started right after the accident and the night's events had replayed in each one, one way or another. But it seemed as though they had only intensified as time went by. As a result, sleep didn't come easily anymore despite how much she needed it. Her doctor prescribed her sleeping pills to get through the night terrors, but Madison felt like by taking them it wasn't facing the reality of what had happened but rather just putting a band-aid over it. Instead, Madison opted to do the breathing exercises that her doctor also prescribed her.

After finishing her breakfast, Madison walked back inside to wash her dishes. Where she was staying was considered a cottage by most people in Toronto, but to people in Meaford it was just another house on the water. It was her uncle and aunt's but, since they had moved to California fifteen years earlier, it had remained empty. When Madison had asked to stay there for the summer, her relatives quickly hired a cleaning lady so it would be livable once she arrived.

It was a modest bungalow, minus its incredible location of being waterfront on Georgian Bay. Facing the water was a porch with a covering veranda and four Muskoka chairs. The sand started beneath the porch steps and led right to the water fifty feet away. Inside, the house was open concept with the kitchen and living room blending into one, the master bedroom and guest bedroom were off to the side of the living room, and the bathroom was beside the front door.

    She'd spent the remainder of yesterday's rain day unpacking her things. Not that she brought very much, but Madison liked to be organized and wanted the cottage to feel as comfortable as possible. The idea of escaping the city suddenly came to her one afternoon when she was feeling low and Madison realized that it was the people around her that were continually making her feel bad about the accident – excluding her parents; they had always been very supportive. However, they were not initially on board with the idea of her moving up north alone, but once she was offered a job at Middleton and Madison had convinced her parents enough that it was what she needed to do, they compromised: they would accept her move to Meaford only if she agreed to call them once a week to check in.

    Exceeding their agreement, Madison had called them yesterday morning when she got home from work. They chatted for half an hour while Madison emptied a cooler and a bag of cupboard essentials her parents had packed for her.

    Madison placed her cereal bowl in the kitchen sink and looked at the clock on the stove – 5:11 AM. There were still close to forty-five minutes before work started, but she wasn't about to sit there waiting around, now wide awake, when she knew her time could be better spent at work. Madison grabbed the lunch she had made the night prior and headed out the door.

"Good morning," Jake said wiping his hands on a rag. He set the rag on the trailer he was hooking up to a golf cart and walked out of the mechanic's door towards her car.

"Morning," Madison responded.

"You know work doesn't start for another forty minutes, right?"

Madison grabbed her extra bags of clothes and rain gear from her backseat. "I couldn't sleep."

"Let me help with those," he said taking one of the bags from her hands.

"Do you always get here this early to set-up?" she asked as they walked into the locker room.

"Usually, but I couldn't sleep either," he repeated with a smile.

Jake returned to the drive shed leaving Madison to organize her locker. It didn't take her long and, after using the washroom, she joined Jake.

"Do you need any help?"

Jake looked over as he finished hooking another trailer to a golf cart. "Sure, if you want to load a couple of walkers onto this that would be great, thanks."

"Are we cutting greens again today together?"

"No, you'll be with Jules today, but leap frogging again with Oskar and Robbie. Speak of the devil, there's Jules now," he said referring to a truck that had pulled into the parking lot.

Madison turned to see Jules flash a big smile as she stepped out of the passenger's side. Even in maintenance clothes - which are baggy and not form fitting at all - Jules was stunning. She had beautiful, long wavy blonde hair that she quickly put into a messy bun as she walked towards them, and stunning hazel eyes. She wore beige pants, a black Middleton golf t-shirt and an un-zipped fleece. Her walk oozed confidence and her genuine, continuous smile made Madison feel like they had known each other for years.

Madison stuck out her hand, but Jules ignored it and gave her a big hug. "I'm so excited to be working with another woman! Not to mention someone who knows what the heck they're doing!"

"Thank you?"

"I asked Jake if we could cut greens together today so that we can have some girl gab!"

Great, Madison thought while trying not to roll her eyes.

"I'm Scott," the man that was driving the truck said shaking her hand.

"So, Jake opens a door on your face and then recruits you to come in early and help him set up?" Jules asked.

"No, I just got here."

Jules didn't look convinced and gave Jake a disapproving look. "Let me go put my lunch in the fridge and then if you're game, we can go out?"

"Jules, it's too ear-" Jake began.

"For sure. I'll just finish loading up these walkers," Madison cut in.

"Great!" Jules looked at Jake. "I like her!"

"Alright that's enough," he said putting his arm affectionately around her and pulling her towards the locker room.

Madison loaded the walkers onto the trailer and put their buckets in the cab of the cart just as Jules returned.

"There's no rain in the forecast for today, so we should be able to finish cutting greens this morning," Jules said locking the driver's side of the walkers' wheels in before getting in the driver's seat. "Okay, but I have to ask. How did you end up here of all places? Don't get me wrong, I love living up here, but young people usually move *away* to find work, not move here *for* work!"

Then why are there so many young people that work here, she wanted to ask but didn't. Honestly, Madison expected to be working with a bunch of old, retired men who would keep to themselves and not care about her. With so many young people close to her age, keeping to herself without coming across as rude was going to be a challenge. Madison realized she was going to have to start telling people something about herself, otherwise their questions would never end and her work comradery with them would plummet.

"You're from around Toronto, right? I think that's what Jake said last night." Jules pressed.

"Yeah, I'm just here for the summer."

"Where are you staying?"

"At my uncle and aunt's cottage."

"Where's their place?"

"Uh, by the water."

"Do you mean that big body of water called Georgian Bay over there?" Jules said sarcastically and pointed in the direction that Georgian Bay was in.

Madison found herself genuinely laughing again for the second time in two days. "Yeah, that one. Their place is near Christie Beach."

"Oh, you're super close! Why were you here so early then? If I lived that close, I'd roll out of bed five minutes before work started."

"Where do you live?"

"Up on the mountain, so it takes a little longer to get here than you, but Jake and Scott live by the water as well. It's so pretty on the water."

"How long have you and Jake been dating?"

Jules looked horrified before slamming on the breaks. "You're joking, right?"

Madison froze. "Yes?"

"Good. While I love the guy, Jake and I have never, nor will we ever, date. Not only do I find him repulsive, but I'm not into incest."

"What?"

"I'm Jake's younger sister, but only by a year and a half!"

"Oh! I just assumed because…well, I don't know."

Jules continued driving. "But, while we are on the subject, I *am* dating Scott."

"That makes more sense because you arrived together this morning," Madison said feeling stupid.

"Scott and I have known each other since we were kids but have only been dating a year; four of those months were in secret, though."

"Why in secret?"

"Well, we weren't sure what Jake would think of us dating because him and Scott are best friends and always have been. It's always been Jake and Scott, Scott and Jake. But he was actually pretty fine with it."

"How did you manage to date secretly if they live together?"

"The three of us hang out a lot, so it wasn't unusual for me to go there for a movie night and stay in their spare room. Then when we started dating, I'd sneak into Scott's room when Jake was asleep and then back into the spare room before he woke up!"

"That sounds like it's out of a movie."

"Right? But nothing is compared to Drew and Evelyn's love story – that's actually movie worthy. Have you met Drew or Ben yet?" When Madison shook her head, Jules continued. "Well, Drew's the Superintendent and Ben's a retired pilot and Drew's engaged to his daughter, Evelyn! They're getting married in July, but they met on the first day of school when they were in grade two. Drew's family had just moved from the city and the day before school started his dog was hit by a car! So, when their teacher noticed how sad he was, she asked him what was wrong. When he told her, Evelyn overheard, walked right up to him, took his hand in hers and said, 'It's going to be okay.' And they've been together ever since!"

"Are you serious?"

"Yeah."

"Does everyone here just date someone they've known since they were kids?"

Jules sighed heavily. "No, sometimes they break up, but that's usually for the best."

Madison felt like there was more to Jules's sigh and response, but knew she was in no position to begin prying.

"Do you golf?" Jules asked pulling off the cart path and parking next to the first hole's green.

"No," Madison lied again. The truth was Madison was an incredible golfer with a ten handicap.

"That's a shame, but you should still come out with us tonight after work! A group of us usually go every Tuesday around twilight." she said unhooking the trailer and unloading the first walker. "Even if you suck, it'll be fun, and you can meet everyone."

"Thanks, but I can't."

"Do you have other plans with your friends up here or something?" Jules joked.

Madison gave a sad smile. "Something like that." She switched the walker on and pulled the start cord before Jules could ask any more questions.

As they continued to cut and leapfrog greens with Oskar and Robbie, Madison didn't have to answer any more questions or talk nearly as much as she thought she might have to with Jules. Not only was Jules a talker and talked enough for them both, but she shared a lot of background information on everyone that worked at Middleton, so Madison was very up to date with all of her coworkers' lives. Once they washed and gassed their walkers, Jake had them cutting fairways together for the rest of the day, starting at the 18th hole and working backwards. By the end of the day, they reached the 10th fairway and, given how busy the golf course was, they were content with the progress they had made.

Madison was surprised to realize she was enjoying working with Jules. She was easy to get along with and she seemed to be a genuine person, someone who told it like it was, and if you didn't like it, tough luck. Despite Madison's initial intentions of not wanting to make friends, Jules was really hard not to like.

The wash bay was at the far end of the drive shed and while Madison and Jules were cleaning their fairway mowers and buckets, someone shouted over their hoses.

"We finally meet!"

She turned to see a guy that was shorter than her, with shaggy brown hair, and the beginnings of what could be a beard in another ten years. Madison shook her head to symbolize she couldn't hear what he had said and turned off her hose.

"I said, 'We finally meet!' I'm Robbie," his voice cracked. "Your face looks better. Wait…I mean after what happened yesterday…."

Jules turned her hose off as well. "What's up, Robbie?"

"What? Oh, nothing." He waved goodbye to them and then stared a little too long at Madison before turning and heading back to the maintenance building.

Jules quickly turned her hose back on and aimed it to spray close to where Robbie was walking. "Pull yourself together, man!" she called out to him. Jules leaned into Madison so she could hear her over her hose. "Are you sure you don't want to come golfing tonight? Robbie will be there, and he might just stare at you some more." She joked. "He's actually a really great guy once you get to know him, and a phenomenal golfer."

"That's what Jake said, too. But, no, I'm good, thanks, though." Madison turned her hose back on and finished cleaning her machine off.

After she put gas in the fairway mower and parked it in the drive shed, she left work quickly before anyone else could invite her to go golfing.

The town of Meaford was only a ten-minute drive away, so Madison decided to head there to go to the grocery and liquor store before heading home and settling in for the evening. Being able to do errands in a town where no one knew her was a relief to Madison. She was not a fan of small talk, especially the kind of small talk people made when there was an oversized elephant in the room. Although it felt like the locals were staring at her, she was sure it was because she looked out of place. Had she been home in Mississauga and doing errands in her parents' neighbourhood, people would be staring at her for an entirely different reason.

She noticed Meaford's quaintness as she drove through town and loved it. Everything from the lampposts, their beautiful town hall and monument in memory of the First World War, to the mom and pop coffee and book shops that lined the main street. Not to mention the town's one and only watering hole, The Leeky Canoe.

After unpacking the groceries, she decided to start her dinner prep since the pork tenderloin needed to marinate. Madison had always loved cooking and, for the last five years, every Tuesday her and Annie took turns cooking for one another.

Sticking with tradition, Madison placed the tenderloin into a zip-lock bag, added some brown sugar, rum, and soy sauce before sealing it and putting it in the fridge. She peeled a few potatoes before cutting them up and placing them in a pot on the stove, ready for when it was time to add water and boil them once she began to cook the meat. She took out a cutting board and chopped up broccoli before scattering it on a cookie sheet and drizzling olive oil, ground pepper, salt, and steak spice over them. She left the tray on top of the stove next to the pot and set a timer on her phone for the marinating meat.

Madison walked out onto the porch and sat in the same Muskoka chair she had earlier that morning. Instantly she was mesmerized by the rolling waves and the quiet noises of the country as time quickly slipped by without her even realizing. The alarm on her phone startled her, and she snapped out of her daze. Feeling a chill, she walked inside and pulled a sweater on before taking out the tenderloin. She turned the oven and stove on and added water to the pot of potatoes. Once the meat was in the oven and the potatoes were boiling, she poured two glasses of red wine.

"Here's to keeping with tradition, Annie. I'm so sorry for everything," she whispered raising her glass to cheers the empty cottage as a tear rolled down her cheek.

Chapter Three

Madison's first week of work at Middleton went better than expected – minus a door being opened on her face and getting rained out on her first day. Drew had her mainly team working with Jules but had given them a variety of jobs that required them to operate several different machines, keeping each day interesting. She had to hand it to Jules, every day she invited Madison to join her, Scott, and Jake after work for drinks at one of their places or to go to the beach but, despite her persistence, Madison always declined. She honestly thought Jules would have given up after the first few days, but she hadn't and came to work each day with her same warm smile. On Friday, however, Madison was able to slip out of work before Jules had the opportunity to invite her anywhere.

It was a beautiful, sunny afternoon and Madison had just finished making lemonade when her cell phone rang.

"Hey Mom," Madison said walking onto the back veranda.

"Hi, honey. I know I'm calling and checking in on you, but sue me, I'm your mother, and we're worried about you. How was your first week of work and being up north?"

Madison affectionately rolled her eyes. "Pretty good. The golf course is stunning, and the people I work with are very nice, but younger than I thought they would be."

"Oh good! You won't be so lonely up there then. How have you been spending your time after work? Have you been hanging out with your co-workers?"

"No, I'm the new weird person from the city. It'll probably be a few weeks before that happens." Madison bit her lip, she hated lying to her mom, but she didn't want to get into why she had been saying no to hanging out with them over the phone. She half expected her mom to call her out on her lie, which she normally did, but this time she let it go.

"Well, why don't you ask them to hang out? You've always been so sociable and you're quite the catch, they'd love you!"

"Thanks, mom. But I'm alright."

"What are your plans for the weekend?"

Madison closed her eyes. "Nothing, which is what I wanted moving up here and is still what I want. Young or old, I didn't come here to make friends, mom, and you and dad both know that."

"We know, but we also know you need something other than work to do. Your time up there shouldn't be a prison sentence, Maddie." Her mom took a deep breath and added softly, "What did you do Tuesday night?"

"Nothing," she replied too quickly and with a hint of attitude. "Sorry. Nothing," she repeated, trying to sound convincing.

When Madison and Annie were little, they always baked cookies or cupcakes after school or on weekends. When they got older and had part-time jobs, they began to expand their baking to cooking and found new recipes each week to do together. Once they were in university and life got busy, they still made hanging out a priority and allocated every Tuesday to rotate between cooking for each other. Despite homework, jobs or boyfriends, they hadn't missed a Tuesday since university started.

"Maddie, remember what the doctor suggested-"

"I know and I don't care what the doctor suggested! Who are they or you to tell me how to deal with my grief?" Madison snapped, but instantly regretted her tone and choice of words. "I'm sorry, mom. I didn't mean that."

A few moments of silence passed before her mother answered, "I've loved and lost, too. Both your father and I have. We just want to make sure you're doing as best as you can be. And I thought we agreed, Tuesdays you should try to find something new to do...."

Madison sighed heavily. "I know. I love you guys too, but I gotta go. I'll call you sometime next week, okay?"

"We love you, too, Maddie."

She ended the call, wiping a tear away with the back of her hand.

When her phone buzzed again, Madison assumed it was her mom having just forgotten to tell her something and didn't even think to check the caller I.D.

"Hiya!" Jules said. "I know you'll probably say no, but you slipped out of work so quickly that I didn't even get the chance to ask! Jake, Scott, and I are going to get wings at The Leeky Canoe - the only pub in town. Do you want to come with us? It's Frrriiidddaaayyy!" she sang.

"Thanks, but-" Madison hesitated because her mother's voice popped into her head: 'your time up there doesn't have to be a prison sentence.'

"You know what, Jules? That actually would be great."

"Really? Yes!" Jules shouted. "We'll come pick you up!"

"No, it's okay, I can just meet you there."

"Don't be silly! You've finally just said yes. We're going to give you the star treatment. What's your address?"

Once Madison told her, Jules said they would pick her up in twenty minutes. Madison went inside to change and stood in front of her closet apprehensively. When she was packing to move to Meaford, she mainly focused on making sure she brought enough work clothes for all weather conditions and comfort clothes for when she wasn't working – not clothes for hanging out with people in. She looked at her limited options and settled on dark blue jeans, a white t-shirt and a grey cardigan.

When she heard a car door slam after fifteen minutes, she peaked out of the bathroom blinds and froze. There stood Jake walking towards her front door, but without Jules or Scott in his truck. "What?" she said quickly spitting the toothpaste out of her mouth.

Madison opened the front door to find Jake standing with his arms up and legs spread in a defensive stance.

"What are you doing?" she asked.

He smiled and relaxed. "On Monday you said you had a retaliation quota and you haven't opened a door on me yet, so I was just taking precaution. How about a truce?" Jake asked extending his hand.

Madison pretended to think about it before replying, "Nope. Where is everyone? Jules made it sound it like we were all driving together?"

"That's what I thought, too, until she told me to come get you."

"Sorry, I told her I could drive-"

Jake waved her off. "That sounded ruder than I intended it to, it's no problem." He leaned in and peaked past her. "Wow, it looks like you have a nice view of the water."

In that moment, Madison caught a whiff of his cologne and her mind buzzed. Whatever kind it was smelled incredible. She took a step back and, without meaning to, couldn't help but notice how handsome he looked. He wasn't wearing a baseball hat, like he had been all week at work, and wore dark blue jeans, a collared and unbuttoned dark navy shirt with a white t-shirt underneath.

"What was that?" Madison asked when she realized Jake was staring at her with a quizzical expression.

"I asked if you were ready to go?" he repeated.

Madison turned and grabbed her purse from the small table by the bathroom door and followed behind him.

"You know the municipality hasn't reported a break-in in, like, ten years," he said when he saw she was locking her door.

"Old city habits die hard," she retorted.

He waited for her by the passenger door. "You're not going to open this on my face, are you?" she asked skeptically as she got another whiff of his cologne.

Jake stared at her with his strikingly blue eyes and smiled slightly. "That was a one-time thing, I promise."

Madison blushed and her heart began to beat faster as she got into his truck.

"So, that's your family's place?" Jake asked driving them away from the cottage. Madison nodded. "Have they had it for a long time?" Madison nodded again. "Is it okay that I'm asking you these questions?" he asked smirking playfully. "Now, before you nod again, I have one more personal question to ask and your answer will determine whether I show you something before meeting up with Jules and Scott at Leeky."

She smiled. "What's the question?"

"Did you ever come up to visit Meaford before this year?"

"What an unusual question," Madison teased. "If I did visit, I was too young to remember. My uncle and aunt bought the cottage and moved to California almost immediately afterwards. My parents' friends are on the other side of the bay, so anytime we'd go north for vacation it was always there rather than here."

"Thank you."

"For what?"

"For not just answering my question, but for telling me a little bit more about yourself."

Madison hadn't even realized she was doing it. There was something about spending more time with him that made her let her guard down.

"It is beautiful on that side of the bay." He continued unaware of her revelation. "But you've been missing out. Not only are we an all-season area, but we don't have the bugs!"

"Do you work for Meaford's tourism board or something when you're not at Middleton?" Madison teased.

"Just wait, you'll see what you've been missing shortly."

Madison was about to object when she found herself smiling and giving in to his charm. They rode the rest of the way in comfortable silence.

At the first set of lights in town, Jake turned left and drove up a sizable hill. At its plateau he turned right into a parking lot and parked his truck overlooking Meaford and Georgian Bay. The view was spectacular, and with the sun beginning to dip in the sky, a gorgeous array of colours spread across the water.

"With a view like this, it's hard to imagine living anywhere other than here. As Meaford's official tourism director I had to say that." He joked. "But it truly is something, isn't it? Even on a dreary day it's stunning. It's a good spot to come when you need to think about things. Here and beside the lighthouse in the harbour because I think there's something very soothing about the sound of water."

Madison wasn't exactly sure why he wanted to show her this view or why he was telling her this, but whatever the reason, she was starting to get the feeling that Jake wasn't like most guys she had met before.

"Thank you for showing me this. You're right; it's gorgeous and I could see how it would be a calming place to come if you needed to think about stuff."

Jake's phone vibrated on the dashboard. "That's probably Jules," he said without even checking. "We should probably get going."

The Leeky Canoe was a revitalized old brick mansion in the heart of downtown Meaford. It had a significantly sized parking lot in the front, and along the building's side, that was surprisingly full. From where Jake parked, Madison could see that there was a large patio out back with a pool table under an awning. Below that there was an even bigger yard in the back that had tables and chairs placed throughout and a gazebo tucked into its back corner.

"The parking lot is so full, yet the patio looks so empty."

"There's a playoff game tonight, so everyone's inside." Jake answered getting out of his truck.

"Really?"

"Not a fan of hockey I take it?" Jake asked as they walked up the side steps.

"I don't mind watching it occasionally, but I'm not the kind of person who would choose to sit inside to watch a game when it's such a beautiful night outside. How about you?"

"I like to keep up with it, but I usually just do that in the mornings with the radio when I drive into work. But it is pretty fun watching games with people that are super into them – like Scott. Are you cool with watching one tonight, though? It'll be more like background noise. We usually talk through the whole thing anyways."

Madison nodded and thought it was very sweet of him to ask. Part of her wondered what he would have suggested had she said she would rather sit outside, though.

When they walked into The Leeky Canoe the bar was packed. Every seat and barstool were taken, and Madison was unsure of how they would find Jules and Scott. Thankfully, Jake seemed to have an idea of where they were seated, and Madison followed him through the crowd. She couldn't help but notice that every so often he looked back to make sure that he hadn't lost her amongst the other patrons. It wasn't long before she spotted Jules waving them over to their booth.

When they reached them, Jake stepped aside to allow Madison to slide into the empty row so she was across from Jules and Jake could be across from Scott.

"Did Merry already come by?" Jake asked.

"Yeah, but we just gave our drink orders and asked that our regular wings be put in once you guys ordered."

Madison was shocked. "You have regular orders here and the waitress remembers them?"

Jules laughed. "Yes, because Leeky is the only place to go for food that's decent without having to drive thirty minutes to the next town. Plus, the waitress, Merry, is a pro."

"Who's this one?" an elderly woman asked setting a tray of drinks on their table and nodding towards Madison. "Nice to see you again, Jake," she said putting her hand on his shoulder.

"Madison Turner. I just started at Middleton," she replied sticking her hand out.

"Are you from the city?"

"How could you tell?"

"You have city written all over you." The woman winked at Jake as she shook Madison's hand.

"And you have country written all over you," she retorted, smiling sweetly.

"Oh, I like her; she's got spunk! I'm Merry. You want your regular, Jake?"

"Yes, please."

"What'll you have, honey?"

"1lb of whatever the hottest wings are, please."

Merry looked over her glasses from her notepad. "Those are really hot."

"Perfect."

Merry's eyes floated to Jake, and she raised her eyebrows. "And to drink?"

"Guinness, please."

"Any of the other num-nuts coming out?" Merry asked.

"Drew and Evelyn might stop by for a drink." Jules offered.

"Their weddin's gonna be somethin', eh?" Merry beamed.

"I can't wait! I've had my dress picked out for months." Jules took Scott's hand in hers. "And you should see this guy in a suit."

"I remember y'all at prom; you guys clean up nice. We best be seeing you there," Merry added looking at Madison.

"Me?" she asked in disbelief.

"Everyone goes to everyone's weddin's here!" Merry said winking before checking on another table.

Jules leaned forward. "Isn't Merry the best? One time when I came here with some friends, she told me about a guy that had just asked her to have a threesome!"

"Really? How old is she?"

"In her late sixties," Scott answered. "Oh, come on!" he shouted at the television. "Bad call, ref!"

Jules continued. "Merry bartends and waitresses everywhere in town. Concerts at the hall, buck n' does, dances, hockey games, weddings, Leeky. You name it, she's there. She knows everything about everyone and has been doing this for years, which is why she's able to remember our regulars. But she's right about Drew and Evelyn's wedding. Evelyn would be beside herself if you didn't come, especially working all summer with us. Everyone from Middleton will be there!"

Merry came back with Madison and Jake's drinks and set them down before quickly leaving.

Jules raised her glass. "Cheers. Here's to making new friends and working with great people."

The conversation between the four of them throughout the night was light, continuously flowing, and they were always joking, bantering, and being sarcastic with one another. Not to mention that, with the hockey game on, there was always something to watch and talk about. Madison realized she was enjoying being in their company, and even getting into watching the hockey game. Jake had been right, with Scott and everyone else so pumped about the playoff game, it had created a contagious atmosphere. Despite the three of them having such a close relationship, they made her feel welcome and as if they'd known her for just as long as they had one another. Any inside joke they had; Jake made sure to explain so Madison didn't feel left out. By the time they were done their wings, she was surprised by how much time had passed without her even noticing.

"Those were really good wings-" Madison began before Scott abruptly cut her off.

"Jake." He nodded towards the front of The Leeky Canoe.

Jake followed Scott's gaze and then shrugged his shoulders before taking a sip of his beer.

Something in Scott's tone had changed. Madison looked to Jules to try to get an idea of what was going on but couldn't read her expression. Whatever had just happened the mood amongst the three of them had shifted.

"He's coming," Scott said calmly.

Jake leaned into Madison and she got another whiff of his cologne, "Everything's fine, but I'm sorry in advance."

"Well, look who I found!" A man slurred as he walked over to their booth. The man had said it so loudly that it had startled Madison and she jumped. He was broad shouldered, at least 6'5, wore a dirty baseball hat and had grease on his arms and hands. "Maybe I should call Becca and let her know you're here? You know she's been trying to get a hold of you, right? Of course, you do because you keep ignoring her calls. All y'all do actually," he added, looking at Jules and Scott.

"Isn't it a bit early to be drunk already, Mike?" Scott asked.

Jake's eyes narrowed at Scott before saying evenly, "Don't mind him, Mike. Why don't you go back to your table and enjoy the game and we'll do the same here?"

Ignoring Jake, Mike placed his hands on their table. "Is this why you've been in hiding?" Nodding to Madison. "You gots yourself a new girlfriend? Man, you sure move fast. Here

Becca's sittin' at home thinking y'all still gonna get married, and now you're seeing some-"

Madison wasn't quite sure how Jake did it but before Mike could finish his sentence, Jake was out of the booth and had grabbed Mike's left arm, twisted it behind his back and had thrown him against a nearby wall. Scott was up equally as quickly and had pushed his way between them.

"Get your hands off me!" Mike hissed.

Jake released him and took several steps back. Mike turned, about to charge, but Scott, broad shouldered and equally as tall as Mike, stood in the way.

"Call her back!" Mike half slurred and half yelled.

"Michael Daniel Smith!" Merry shouted walking towards them. Not only was she triple his age but at least two feet shorter than him, but that didn't seem to deter her at all. "Youse better leave right now! There was no trouble until you showed up. Go on now! Get!"

Mike's heavy breathing slowed and, at the sound of Merry's voice, he seemed to have snapped out of his trance. "This isn't over!" he added, staring at Jake before leaving.

"Alright, nothing to see here people!" Scott yelled, clapping his hands.

Jake slowly slid back into their booth. "I'm sorry for that, Madison. I don't know about you guys, but I'm ready to go." He pulled his wallet out and put enough cash on the table for everyone's meals and drinks.

Once the initial shock had washed over Madison, she rummaged through her purse looking for her wallet as Scott and Jules slid out of their side of the booth.

"No, it's on me," Jake said putting his hand over hers. "I opened a door on your face, and you just had to witness that. Please, it's the least I can do."

Madison was about to object when she noticed the sadness in his eyes. "Okay, thank you."

As soon as they were outside, Jules took Jake's arm and guided him away from the parking lot. "Can I speak to you for a moment?" she asked him rhetorically.

Once they were out of earshot, Scott turned to Madison, "Mike's a piece of work and can't mind his own business."

"I'm in no position to judge or ask any questions."

"Well, it's no secret what's going on between them, the whole town knows, but it's not my story to tell."

"That's fair," Madison said, yet her mind was racing. Who was Mike? Who was Becca? Was Jake engaged? If so, why wouldn't he have said something? If not, how come? Why was Jake ignoring Becca's calls? Why were Jules and Scott ignoring Becca's calls? What the hell was all of that even about? Why do I seem care so much?

They stood waiting by Jake's truck in silence until Jake and Jules finished their conversation and were walking back towards them.

"I'm sorry that the first night you decide to come and hang out with us you got to meet that chump!" Jules said and gave Madison a tight hug goodbye. "Have a wonderful weekend. Let's try hanging out again sometime next week, okay?"

Scott took Jules's hand and wrapped it around his side before draping his arm across her shoulders as they walked towards his truck.

Jake turned and opened the passenger door for Madison. Her heart clenched when their eyes met, and she saw his sad smile. The drive back to her family's cottage was silent but, considering they had only known each other a week and the altercation that had just happened, it wasn't uncomfortable.

When they pulled into her driveway, Jake instantly put his truck into park and got out. "I'll walk you to your door," he said. His gentlemanly gesture didn't feel forced and Madison honestly felt like him walking her to her door was just part of his character. But most guys she knew weren't as chivalrous which she thought said so much more about Jake because even when he was clearly upset about what had just happened, he would still walk her to her door.

He slowed and stopped at the end of the front path. "I'm sorry again for what happened tonight. That wasn't how I hoped the night would go."

How did you hope the night would go? Madison couldn't help but wonder. "Look, I don't know the history, obviously, and I don't need to know, but you have nothing to be sorry about. You tried to diffuse the situation before it escalated, and it only got that way because of that Mike guy, not you." Jake was looking at his shoes and Madison couldn't tell if he was struggling with whether to tell her more or was just unsure of how to end the night. "Do you want to come in?" she asked, surprising herself yet again.

"No," he quickly replied. "But thank you. I'll see you Monday." He gave a half smile before turning and walking back to his truck.

Madison found herself standing there, watching him drive away but wishing he had stayed.

Chapter Four

From working early mornings at a golf course for so many years, Madison found it difficult to sleep past sunrise – even on her days off. She got used to being efficient throughout her mornings so that by the time most people were just waking up, Madison already had a head start to her day. When she wasn't working, Madison would either get her daily exercises in or, if she was feeling like having a lazy morning, make a pot of coffee, curl back into bed and continue reading the latest book that had captivated her.

However, with her first Saturday off in Meaford Madison was feeling anything but lazy. She had done a little research before moving there about things to do in the area and hiking had come up often. While Meaford was surrounded by Georgian Bay on one side, the other side was surrounded by ski hills that had hiking trails throughout them in the off season. Her plan this morning was to hike one of them in time to catch the sunrise.

It was a brisk morning, so Madison wore thick running tights, a Smartwool long-sleeve, and put her Patagonia windbreaker over top. She grabbed a banana, a few granola bars and her coffee, before heading out the door.

Even though it was late spring, and the days were getting warmer, the mornings could still be quite cold. However, Madison knew that once she started to hike, the slight chill she was feeling would go away.

After driving twenty minutes, Madison pulled her car into the first ski hill's parking lot. She fastened a headlamp to her head that she had found in one of the front hallway drawers and started her ascent. As she walked past the clubhouse, she spotted a dirt road that appeared to go up a ski run. Madison decided to follow it assuming it was a maintenance road that would lead her right to the top. Before the road went too far, she passed a trail map and scanned it to see where she was. Madison was relieved to see that the road that led up the ski hill was a blue colour – meaning it wouldn't be too steep.

The climb was peaceful and serene. The dirt road slowly wound its way up to the very top and only had a couple of minor steep sections. As she hiked, she breathed deeply and hungrily for the fresh air and as she worked harder and her legs burned, she could feel her mind clearing.

When Madison made it to the peak, she climbed onto one of the chairlift platforms and sat with her legs stretched out, facing Georgian Bay. She turned her headlamp off and stared at the sky as the stars began to fade. Madison was struck by how beautiful the night sky was without all the light pollution she was used to seeing in the city.

She closed her eyes and practiced the mindfulness breathing exercises her doctor had suggested through deep, slow, and steady breaths. When she felt ready to open her eyes, she saw the first glitters of light in the distance. Pink, purple, and orange melted together creating a gorgeous, mesmerizing sunrise. It started subtly, but, bit by bit, Georgian Bay became illuminated, and somewhere in Madison's heart, she felt the beauty of this moment was Annie sending her a message. Unlike the angry Annie that always appeared in Madison's nightmares, which she knew was solely a product of her own subconscious, this tranquility among her heartache had Annie written all over it.

With her mind clear, Madison knew it was moments like this or the quiet ones where she was sitting on the verandah overlooking the water, that were going to help her be able to heal. She knew the nightmares and self-doubt would be a battle, but the more clarity she was able to get, the easier those would be to conquer.

Even though Madison had only been living in Meaford a week, since she'd been there, she was already beginning to feel like things might be okay. She closed her eyes and relished the warmth that the sun brought.

Madison had left her cell phone in the car, so she had no idea how long she had been sitting, admiring the view. But, when her stomach began to rumble, she decided it was time to begin her descent and get some breakfast.

It quickly turned into a warm morning, and by the time she got in her car she had to roll its windows down to let the heat that was building escape. Rather than turning off the highway to go home, Madison decided to keep driving towards Meaford. She had really appreciated Jake showing her the lookout yesterday, but he had also mentioned the harbour rocks by the lighthouse and Madison felt compelled to check it out.

She drove through town and stopped at the first mom and pop breakfast restaurant she found. Getting a bagel and another coffee, she could see the water from its windows and decided to leave her car parked where it was and walk to the harbour.

Its parking lot had a few people in it working on their sailboats, doing last-minute things before they would be put in the water for the season.

She walked along the pier towards the breakwall that would eventually lead her to the lighthouse Jake had mentioned. The breakwall was made up of massive rocks with flat tops that were clearly strategically placed so people could walk to the end and back safely. She saw a few people fishing from the bottom of the breakwall, but other than that it was a very quiet morning.

However, when she got closer to the lighthouse, she could see that there was someone leaning against it reading a book. She decided that she wouldn't walk too closely to the person, so as not to disrupt them, and as she was about to turn around to head back to her car she froze.

"Hey Jake! Beautiful morning, isn't it?"

"Hey Robert! Hey Jayne! I couldn't have asked for anything better. You guys stay safe out there."

Adjacent to the lighthouse was a coastguard station and a couple of its officers were leaving the harbour in one of their boats.

"Will do!" Robert replied tipping his hat first at Jake and then at Madison.

Jake followed Robert's gaze and a big smile spread across his face when he saw her. "Madison?" he asked getting up.

"Hey," she said uneasily, suddenly nervous. "Sorry. I didn't mean to disturb you. I didn't even realize that was you."

"You're not disturbing me at all. I'm just a little surprised to see you. What are you doing here?"

"I was just exploring. What about you?"

He shrugged his shoulders. "I just needed to think about a few things. Scott and I live just over there actually, so it's much closer to come here than the lookout." Madison looked across the harbour to a small bungalow that he was pointing to.

"You're up pretty early for your day off?" she inquired.

"I could say the same about you."

Madison felt herself blushing and shrugged. "I'm a morning person. What are you reading?"

"Ken Follett's *Winter of the World*. It's part of a trilogy that's taking me forever to get through."

"I think my favourite was the third one: *Edge of Eternity*."

"You've read this series?" Jake asked in disbelief.

Madison nodded. "And *Pillars of the Earth* and its sequel. Have you read those?"

"Yeah! Did you know they made a mini-series out of it?"

Madison nodded. "I thought it was okay…."

Jake's eyes were extraordinarily blue especially in the morning light, and Madison suddenly felt self-conscious.

"I'm out of coffee," he finally said bending over to pick up his thermos and the cushion he had been sitting on. "Do you want to come over for a cup?"

"Oh, no, thank you. This is my second already," she said jiggling the thermos she had the restaurant refill.

"I'll walk back with you then. Were you out running or something this morning?"

"No, not this morning. Just a hike up one of the skill hills."

"Oh, *just* a hike up one of the ski hills?" He teased, mocking her.

"Are you making fun of me?"

"I would never." He smirked. "Are you sure you don't want a little more coffee? Jules and Scott probably have another pot going already."

"Is it weird having your best friend and your sister date?" she asked but immediately regretted it upon seeing his surprised look. "Oh dear. You don't have to answer that. I'm sorry-"

He laughed and waved her off. "It's okay. I like you asking me questions."

She felt herself blushing again. Well, in that case, I have a whole whack of questions that I'd like answers to from last night, she thought but didn't voice.

Jake continued, "It does get a little weird sometimes. I welcome excuses to leave the house, and I'm sure they welcome excuses for me to leave as well. But how about some water instead? You're probably parched after your hike? Before you say no, just say yes," He smiled.

"Am I that predictable?" Madison laughed.

"Yes," he replied with emphasis. "Jules made muffins last night, and Scott and I can't eat them all. You'd really be doing us a favour."

"Well, I do like muffins…."

"That sounds like a yes to me," He grinned.

Their house was a neat bungalow that had a very Cape Cod feel with light grey board and batten on its side with white trim. Inside it was exactly what Madison would have imagined a house that two male best friends were living in would look like. They had their road and mountain bikes hanging from S hooks in the large, open front foyer, as well as skateboards, racquets, basketballs, gloves, helmets, and bike pumps. The hallway curved to the left and opened into a large common space with the kitchen to the right. Along the back-living room wall were sliding doors that led to a deck. Parallel to that were the bedrooms and a bathroom with their television hanging on the wall between their doors. Across from where she stood was a massive bookcase.

"Wow, that's beautiful!" Madison said as soon as she rounded the front hall corner and spotted it.

"Is that Madison I hear?" Jules said getting up from the breakfast buffet. "What an amazing surprise! Would you like a coffee? Or a muffin? I made some yesterday."

Madison walked over to the bookcase and began scanning its titles. "Both would be lovely, thank you."

"They're all Jake's books," Scott said walking towards Madison with her coffee and muffin.

"Really?"

"Yeah, he's the philosopher and bookworm between us," he added.

"He also built the bookshelf from old barn board," Jules contributed.

"Alright, that's enough," Jake said waving Jules and Scott off.

"What?" Jules asked innocently.

"What's your favourite book?" Madison inquired.

"That's a loaded question, but I think I would have to say *War and Peace* by Leo Tolstoy."

"I can't say I've read that, but I did see the miniseries and I know they're not the same, but it was pretty good. I see you're into WWII history. Have you read *The Nightingale* or *Sarah's Key*?"

"I did but only because Jules suggested them. They were great, though. What's your favourite book?"

"Easy, *To Kill A Mockingbird* by Harper Lee."

"Did you read its sequel?"

Madison nodded finishing her muffin. "But it wasn't comparable."

"Sorry for interrupting," Scott said holding the coffee pot. "Would you like some more coffee, Madison?"

"No, thank you. I should actually get going." she said walking into their kitchen with her mug. "Where should I put this?"

"Just leave it in the sink, that's fine," Jules said.

"Are you sure?" Jake asked dismayed. "You just got here."

"Yeah. It was nice running into you though, Jake," She smiled at him before looking at Jules and Scott who were looking amused. "The muffin was delicious, thank you. Enjoy the rest of your weekend."

"I'll walk you out."

Madison suddenly felt butterflies in her stomach as Jake walked behind her.

"Maybe I'll run into you again sometime this weekend?" he said, leaning against the front door's frame.

Madison turned and smiled at the bottom of the front steps. "Maybe."

Jake watched her walk back towards town, only turning to go back inside once she was out of view.

When he got back into the kitchen, both Scott and Jules shared the same smirk.

"What?"

Chapter Five

Madison's second week at Middleton seemed to go by very quickly. Drew had her working mainly with Jules or by herself, but still changed what she was doing almost daily which continued to keep work engaging. However, by her third week a multiple day storm had rolled into Meaford making working conditions less than desirable. Late Sunday evening, it began to rain torrentially again and continued until Monday afternoon. Everyone was told to stay home and, despite Jules inviting her to breakfast, Madison used the extra day and the miserable weather to be alone. She sat on the back porch for most of the day with blankets wrapped around her watching the storm ravage over Georgian Bay.

The following day's weather was a bit better and she was able to work for at least three hours pumping bunkers or cleaning up debris left from the storm's winds. Although, after a while, it became redundant because the winds picked up again and whatever had been cleared previously was instantly replaced by newly broken branches.

By Wednesday, though, the weather was good enough that she had a full days' work, but it remained surprisingly cold for almost going into summer meaning the fair-weather golfers stayed home and Middleton was a ghost town.

They were able to cut some areas on the golf course, but most were too wet and the machines' weight would damage the grass. Instead, everyone continued to pump water from the sand traps, pick up debris or rope off areas where the ground was water-logged to protect the grass and allow it to grow back.

By the end of the day, Madison's socks and shoes were completely soaked and she was very thankful that she lived only around the corner and that having a hot shower would be imminent.

"Knock, knock." a woman said walking through the side maintenance door. "Drew? Dad?"

Madison was sitting on a work bench changing her socks and peered around the locker room corner. The woman was tall with wavy, long blonde hair and a slightly crooked smile that was endearing. She wore long khaki pants, a purple wind breaker, and a navy, pin-striped polo golf shirt.

"I don't think either of them are here, but they should be in any minute. I'm Madison," she said standing up to greet her.

"Madison! It's so nice to finally meet you! I've heard so many wonderful things from Drew. I'm Evelyn, his fiancé and Ben's daughter."

Madison shook her outstretched hand. "It's nice to meet you, too. Congratulations on your upcoming wedding!"

"Thank you! I really hope the weather holds off. No more of these fluke storms. Drew extended the invitation to you already, right?"

"He did and that's kind of you both, but I don't want to impose on your big day."

"Nonsense. You work here now and will be working every day with my fiancé and my father. Not to mention Jules and Jake are just smitten with you, so you must!"

Madison's heart jumped. Jake was smitten with her?

"Hey! Someone's ready for golf!" Drew said walking into the locker room and kissing Evelyn on the cheek. "You guys already met I'm guessing?"

"Yes, and I was just telling her how she has to come to our wedding."

"Definitely," Drew agreed. "Not only do we want you there, but it's what we do up here. Everyone goes to everyone's wedding."

"Weddings up here do sound fun." Madison offered but was still unconvinced she wanted to attend. It wasn't that she didn't want to go, it was just she barely knew them. Even so, it seemed everyone was telling her that it was common for people to go to every single wedding in Meaford regardless of how well they knew the bride and groom. Madison didn't want to offend anyone by not going, but, thankfully, she still had lots of time to decide before their big day.

"Do you have baked goods in those Tupperware containers?" Drew asked Evelyn.

"I do. Skor chocolate chip cookies to eat while we golf and banana chocolate chip muffins for everyone tomorrow morning."

"You're too good to us, thank you," he said, kissing her cheek again while taking the cookies.

"I should put a note on these muffins, so people don't eat them now," Evelyn said walking towards one of the lunch tables that had notepads and pens sitting on top of it in a basket. "Are you coming golfing?" Evelyn asked.

"You guys are golfing *today*? It's kind of chilly out there."

Evelyn looked at the wet socks Madison had in a bag next to her. "I have dry and warm socks if you want to borrow some? It might not feel as cold once your feet are warm? But today's weather is why it'll be the best time to go – we can take our time and not have to worry about our group slowing actual paying golfers down."

"Thank you, but I can't."

"That's too bad. Are you not a golfer?"

"No." The lie continues.

"Well, I'm not either so I hope that's not what's stopping you! We could be amateurs together!"

"And why can't you come this time?" Jake inquired standing in the door frame between the locker room and maintenance shed.

"I need to get some groceries. Plus, I don't have clothes or clubs."

He smiled. "We can set you up with clothes and clubs if that's what's truly stopping you. We're not teeing off for another hour, so there's lots of time to get those groceries too."

"You would make an even eight," Evelyn added before Madison could object any further.

Madison felt slightly cornered, but Evelyn's words continued to buzz in her head, '…Jake is just smitten with you,' and Madison found herself wanting to find out exactly what that meant.

"Okay," She relented. "I'm in."

"Let's just remember how lucky we are to be golfing at such a fine golf course and in such a large group, especially on a day like today. If it were any other group, we would have turned them away. And let's be mindful of where we step and drive our carts too to not make more work for ourselves," Drew announced to the group of Middleton workers as they stood on the first tee deck. "Throw a club in."

"I'll toss them!" Robbie shouted kneeling towards the pile.

Jules leaned over to Madison. "$20 says he's going to try to pair your clubs together 'accidentally.'"

"Lucky me," she replied sarcastically.

When Robbie was done throwing clubs, he picked his and its pairing up and walked towards Madison, smiling.

"Thanks, man," Scott said interjecting and taking the other golf club from Robbie's hands.

Robbie's smile faded. "That's not yours," he said, taking it back.

"Yes, it is." Scott said grabbing it again.

Robbie turned to see Jake handing Madison her club. "Unbelievable!"

"Amateur," Jules winked walking past him towards her partner, Evelyn.

Jake strapped their golf bags to the back of their cart. "Do you want to drive?"

"All you," She smiled.

"We usually play something called, 'best ball' between cart partners." he said, sitting in the driver's seat. "Whoever shoots best between us, Jules and Evelyn, Scott and Robbie, and Oskar and Drew, the partners will shoot from that ball for the next shot, and then whoever has the better ball between them from that shot, will shoot from there and so on…."

Listening to Jake explain best ball to her was very sweet. He, of course, thought she had never played golf before and didn't understand the game, and Madison knew that was her own fault. Now that they were golfing, though, she wasn't sure how long she was going to be able to keep up the 'not-a-golfer' charade. Everyone was going to be able to quickly see that Madison's golfing ability wasn't just beginner's luck.

"No pressure to do well," Jake continued. "We just have fun with it, but if you would like any pointers, just let me know."

"Thanks," Madison replied uneasily. "Okay, listen, I have a confession," she blurted out.

He raised his eyebrows. "Is it juicy?"

"I'm a golfer."

"That's your confession? No offense, but I was kind of hoping it was going to be better than that."

"I'm sorry I lied about it. I just…well, to be honest, I didn't come up here to make friends and when you asked if I golfed, I thought it would just be easier if I lied and said no."

"…So that we wouldn't ask you to hang out or golf?"

"Yeah."

"And yet here you are. I think it's safe to say that we charmed you, Madison."

She couldn't help but smile. "Something like that."

"But I think the bigger question I have is why did you move up here and not want to make friends?"

Madison sighed and was about to give an answer when Jake continued.

"I remember you said that you didn't want to talk about you on your first day and I get the feeling that's still what you want. But I also get the feeling that you're a bit torn because you kind of like us?"

She smiled again. "Only a little, though."

Jake returned her smile and drove them to the first tee deck.

It felt good to have corrected one of her lies and tell Jake the truth, even if it was only a little bit of it. She was slightly awestruck that he had been so understanding about it, too. Not to mention that he had called her out on something she had said, but not in a rude or prying way.

"How long have you played golf for?"

"Since I started working at Ruby Lewis…nine summers ago."

"What's your handicap?"

"Ten. Yours?"

Jake parked their cart behind Jules and Evelyn's. "Mine's ten on a good day!"

"Who's teeing off first between you two?" Jules asked standing in front of their cart as she got her driver out of her bag.

"Madison," Jake answered quickly. "Hey, why don't we play for something?"

"Jake, it's her first time. Let's not get super competitive about it." Jules said.

"Oh, come on, it could be fun. What do you think, Madison?" he asked.

"Do you guys normally play for something?"

"Yes," they replied in unison.

"Well, if it's something you normally do then, sure."

Jules took a couple practice swings on the tee deck. "Okay, how about if Evelyn and I win, you guys cook us dinner Friday night? But if we lose, we'll cook you dinner."

Jake raised his eyebrows at Madison, leaving the decision up to her.

"You're on," she confirmed.

Madison wasn't sure how good of a golfer Jules was, but seeing her practice swings she could tell she had a very strong drive and began to think that this could be a very tight game.

Madison walked onto the tee deck and, after teeing her ball, took a few practice swings herself. When she first took up golf, she had convinced Annie to join her. That summer they went out twice a week and, before they knew it, they were both half decent players. Madison took it a bit more seriously while Annie only stuck with it because she realized a lot of hot guys were golfers. Between them it became slightly competitive, but as soon as Annie saw a good-looking guy, she pretended that she didn't know how to play in hopes they would help her. Often, they did and this drove Madison nuts because she was the complete opposite and loved competition – especially between sexes, and when the men couldn't stand women being better than them.

Driving a golf ball had always been one of the strongest parts of Madison's game, yet as she stood on the tee deck with everyone's eyes on her, she felt nervous. She took a deep breath before swinging and sending her golf ball flying. The first hole was a par four that dog-legged left, and she watched with an inward smirk as her golf ball followed its curve and landed less than fifty yards from the green.

"Wow!" Jules exclaimed.

"And she's *not* a golfer? I think I need to stop coming out with you guys then," Evelyn added.

"We get to pick the dinner we want you guys to cook for us, right?" Jake asked Jules while teeing his ball.

"Wait a second, did you know about this?" she asked, referring to Madison's golfing ability.

He smiled innocently. "Know about what?"

Jake's drive landed roughly ten yards short of Madison's, and Jules another five from his.

As they drove to their balls, Jake leaned in. "I'm pretty sure Jules thought the real competition would be between me and her for this dinner, so I think they're reevaluating their strategy. We should probably figure out what meal we'd like them to cook us. What's your favourite dinner?"

Madison laughed. "Let's not get ahead of ourselves here, you haven't seen my short game yet." She paused. "But I like everything, I'm not picky, especially if someone else is cooking for me."

"Do you like to cook?"

"I love it. How about you?"

"I do. Growing up, our mom made sure I was in the kitchen as much as Jules - if not more."

"Your mom sounds amazing."

"She was."

"Oh, Jake, I'm sorry-"

"It's fine, you didn't know," he said waving his hand. "She died twelve years ago from breast cancer."

"I'm sorry for your loss…."

As Madison said those five words something inside of her clicked. For months people had been saying that to her and Madison couldn't be more sick of hearing it. But upon Jake telling her of his loss, it was a knee-jerk reaction: something people automatically say when they discover someone has lost someone special to them. In a fleeting moment, Madison suddenly felt like she wished Jake knew about Annie. Not in a your-mom-died-and-so-did-my-best-friend kind of way, but in a revealing-a-vulnerable-part-of-yourself kind of way. She knew this wasn't the time nor the place to mention it, but she felt for the first time that she *wanted* to talk about Annie's death with someone.

After Jules and Evelyn had taken their next shots, Jake drove parallel to his golf ball and picked it up with his left hand while his right hand remained on the steering wheel and his right foot on the gas. "Excellent shot," he said as he drove next to where Madison's lay and dropped his ball next to it.

"Thanks, yours was pretty good, too."

They both stepped out and walked towards their golf bags. Taking out their pitching wedges, Jake let Madison shoot first. Her ball landed close to the pin, but his rolled closer.

"Looks like this win is going to be a team effort," she said.

Jules' ball landed on the edge of the approach, close enough that she and Evelyn would be able to use their putter rather than pitching wedge if they wanted. Despite Evelyn saying she wasn't good at golf; she was good at putting and was able to sink their ball in two shots allowing them to make par, with Madison and Jake scoring a birdie.

"Have you lived in Meaford your whole life?" Madison asked as they drove to the second tee.

"Before I answer that, am I allowed to ask you a question in return?"

"Yes, but on the condition that I don't have to answer."

"Then neither do I, but deal. Yes, I was born and raised here and have lived here my entire life, except when I went to the University of Guelph for golf course management. Where are you from?"

"Born and raised in Mississauga except when I went to Ryerson for journalism; I lived downtown first year. I was back home living with my parents before moving up here, though."

"Ah, that's why you moved up here. No offense to your parents, but it's hard living with them again after you've been out on your own. There must be lots of jobs in the city for journalism, though, or do you have other plans?"

While he wasn't entirely wrong with her reason for moving up north, Jake wasn't entirely right either. Again, Madison didn't think it was the right time or place to bring Annie up, so she continued to let him believe that's why she moved.

"There are a lot of opportunities, but yes, I'm keeping my options open." Madison also didn't see the point in revealing that, had things worked out differently, she could have been going to The University of Guelph in the fall for the same program he had already completed. The option to attend the following year was still open to Madison because she had only deferred her acceptance.

As Jake became more interested in her and continued to ask questions, Madison realized that if she didn't start telling him the truth soon, the lies would only get bigger and worse. Even though they were white lies, she was beginning to feel bad about them and trapped. She made the conscious decision that when the right opportunity arose, she would tell him the complete truth.

"So is your plan to head back to the city at the end of the summer or stay up here…?"

"That's two questions in one," she coyly said.

"You got me, but I'm only asking because I know Drew would love it if you stayed throughout the fall, and if not there will definitely be a job for you here next summer if you wanted to come back."

Something inside made Madison hope he wasn't trying to find out her future plans solely because of work. "Thanks, I'll keep that in mind."

The next seven holes proved to be a tighter competition between her and Jules than she expected. While Madison usually drove further than her, Jules's short game was slightly better than Madison's. By the ninth hole there was a seven-point difference between the duos. Madison and Jake were getting birdies on every hole and Jules was mainly getting boogies, with a couple of pars.

While they played, Madison was beginning to think that Jules had something to do with hers and Jake's clubs getting paired together. She wasn't sure how she could have done it with Madison standing right there and Robbie throwing them, but Jules had made a couple of comments as their game progressed to lead Madison to believe that she had. To be honest, Madison was thankful that she was golfing with Jake because she was genuinely enjoying getting to know him. They surprisingly had more in common than she thought, and he was easy to talk to. He listened with intent and purpose when she spoke, and when he looked at her, it was like she was the only person on the golf course.

"We have a tradition with the ninth hole that we all tee off and play it together," Jake said pulling up to its tee deck.

"I would just like to say that I think my partner should have gotten a mulligan on every hole because she is carrying our team," Evelyn stated as they parked beside Madison and Jake. "It's really two against one here."

"No way!" Jake laughed. "A delicious dinner is on the line, and I can't wait to have some lovely home cooking."

"I cook for you all the time!" Jules said.

"You cook for your boyfriend and his roommate all the time," Jake corrected with a smile.

"What do you think, Madison?" Evelyn asked.

"How about we scratch the previous score, start fresh, and you get a free mulligan, if you want, on this hole."

"What?" Jake exclaimed.

"I think that's a great idea!" Jules and Evelyn said in unison.

"Who's winning?" Scott inquired pulling his cart up behind them.

"Don't get me started," Jake jokingly sulked.

"Everything's riding on this hole!" Jules announced.

The ninth hole was 387 yards from the cobalt blocks, with a sharp dogleg to the left and a creek meandering through the fairway. Madison knew she could drive it over the water feature with ease and guessed Jules would play it safe, aiming before it to avoid landing in the water. She then figured both teams would end up on the green from their second shot, and that it would all come down to putting.

When each of them drove their balls, they landed exactly where Madison had predicted they would, as did their second shots. By this point, Drew, Oskar, Scott, and Robbie had stopped caring about their game and were completely enraptured in the ninth hole competition between the other four.

Once they got to the green, everyone was so quiet that it could have been The Masters. The three serious golfers knelt to find the right lines for their putts. All eyes were on Jules as their balls were furthest away. She took a couple of practice putts before finally stepping closer to her ball. At first it looked like her putt was going to go in, which would give her and Evelyn a birdie but, at the last second, it turned to the right and swayed away from the hole.

"That's okay. We still have Evelyn's putt, and I can use that mulligan," Jules said smiling.

Evelyn placed her ball next to Jules' ball marker. Her carefree attitude for the competition was radiating off her because she immediately lined her putter up and not even checking a line or taking practice swings, putted.

"Oh my god, Evelyn!" Jules shouted as they all watched her ball sink in the hole. "What a putt! If they don't get this in, that means we win!"

Jake high fived Evelyn. "Incredible putt!" He put his ball down and leaned into Madison. "So, which team cooks dinner if we sink this and it's a tie?"

"Potluck dinner?"

Jake thought for a moment and whispered. "That works, but if I sink this, will you have lunch with me on Sunday?"

Her heart skipped a beat. Was Jake asking her out on a date or was he was just being friendly? Madison had just told him that she hadn't moved to Meaford to make friends so he must know then that that means she certainly didn't move there to start dating someone either. "Like a date?"

"Or just two people sharing a meal together?"

"Okay," she whispered.

Jake knelt to check his line and took a few practice swings before inching closer to his ball. What if he didn't sink his putt? Would that mean lunch is off? Realizing she really *did* want to have lunch with him, Madison closed her eyes when she saw him backswing. Within seconds, she heard the kerplunk of the ball and everyone giving him praise.

When she opened her eyes, Jules was in front of her sticking out her hand. "I think we're going to have to golf more often. It's not every day you meet a lady who's as good as you are."

Madison shook her hand. "Thank you. I should have told you that I golfed when you asked me originally, I'm sorry."

"That's okay. New town, new people, I get wanting to keep to yourself."

"So, who makes dinner now?" Drew asked putting his arm around Evelyn. "It was a tie, right?"

"That's right. Why don't we all bring something and have a potluck?" Evelyn suggested.

"Madison was thinking the same thing and I think that's a great idea." Jake said shaking his sister's hand.

Finding herself already looking forward to the evening, Madison asked, "What can I bring?"

Chapter Six

Just as quickly as the storm had rolled into Meaford earlier in the week it had left, bringing sunny skies and warm weather. Madison reevaluated her clothing options for the ninth hole potluck dinner and wasn't content with any of it. So, when she went grocery shopping for the salad she was going to bring, she also stopped at a few clothing stores downtown Meaford. The second shop she went into had a sale on for dresses and after finding three she liked, she bought the first two and got the third half priced. Two of the three dresses were casual summer dresses, so she decided to wear one for their potluck dinner Friday and the other one for her Sunday lunch with Jake. The third dress she bought was a bit of a fancier one so if she ended up deciding to go to Drew and Evelyn's wedding, she at least had something she could wear now.

Giving herself one final look over in the bathroom mirror, Madison smoothed out her dress. She thought she looked good and was happy with her choice to buy the blue and white pinstriped sundress. Not that tonight was a date or anything, because Jules and Evelyn were going to be there too, but she was feeling very happy and confident as she picked up the goat cheese and walnut salad she had made off the kitchen counter and headed out the door. The four of them had decided yesterday at work what everyone would bring: Jake said he would take care of the main while Jules would make an appetizer, and Evelyn would make the dessert.

Madison arrived at Jake's exactly on time only to find his truck in the driveway – not Jules's or Evelyn's. Maybe they were just running late or maybe Drew dropped them off?

As she approached Jake's house, Madison could hear him laughing through their screen door. She gave a light knock.

"Hello?" she called opening the door and stepping inside.

"Hey," Jake called as he walked from inside toward their foyer, but immediately stopping upon seeing her. "Wow, you look fantastic."

Madison's face grew warm as she noticed how good he also looked. Jake was wearing a fitted dark blue collared shirt that had small white shapes on it and beige khaki shorts. "Thank you. You do, too. I heard you laughing, what's so funny?"

"Just Jules and Evelyn. Come in, I'll show you. Here let me take that," he said grabbing the salad from her hands.

"Are they on their way?"

"They were already here."

Madison walked into his kitchen to see a brie dip and chocolate cake sitting on the buffet. "Are they coming back?"

"I don't think so. They came over earlier than expected and after we had a drink and I hopped in the shower, they took off. I assumed they were out on the deck or something but then was reading their note when you'd knocked. They also left a couple bottles of wine."

Madison's heart began to race. "What?" This was certainly beginning to feel more like it was a date now.

"I know this isn't what we initially planned, but would you still like to stay?"

"Of course," she said as the butterflies started.

Jake smiled. "Great! Your salad looks incredible by the way. Can I get you something to drink?"

"I'll have a glass of wine, please."

"Red or white?"

"Red."

"So, what's in the homemade salad dressing you were telling us about?" he asked pouring them both a glass.

"Olive oil, balsamic vinegar, Dijon mustard, and maple syrup."

"Maple syrup?"

"Yes, it's delicious, trust me."

"Family recipe?"

"Sort of. It's my best friend's recipe."

"Cheers to your best friend's recipe then," Jake said as they clinked their wine glasses. Jake took the lid off the brie dip and they both had a seat on the buffet stools. "How was your day?"

Despite working at the same place, Madison and Jake didn't really see each other so them talking about their days wasn't redundant or strange. Madison recounted her struggles of pumping out the remaining bunkers before Jake recapped his day of tackling a broken irrigation line.

"What kind of pipelines are underground?"

"Polyethylene."

"Polyvinyl Chloride is better. Polyethylene might be cheaper than polyvinyl, but it's weaker."

Jake stared at her surprised. "No offense, but how do you know that?"

This was it, she thought. This was the right time and place to confess that she was practically the assistant superintendent at Ruby Lewis and that she could be going into the same program at Guelph that Jake had been in.

"That's almost exactly what I told Drew!" Jake continued. "He said that they had to stick to the budget, and by getting polyvinyl pipelines it would put them over." He looked at his watch and got up from the stool. "Let me just get the barbeque started."

"Can I help with anything?" Madison asked as Jake slipped out the back door.

"Well, I was hoping we could eat outside, but it's getting kind of cold. How do you feel about sitting on the floor in the living room and eating at the coffee table? Would that be okay in your dress?"

Again, Madison was stuck by his thoughtfulness. "Yeah, I can set it up. Just tell me where everything is."

Jake pointed out the cupboards Madison would need before stepping outside to light the barbeque. After cleaning off its grill, he popped back inside to grab the steaks and vegetable kebabs from the fridge. She stole the odd glance at him while he managed the barbeque and even thought she caught him doing the same at her while she set the table. Or was he? Madison was unsure if she was beginning to imagine things because of wishful thinking. She poured them more wine, consciously knowing this would be her last glass so she could drive home later.

"Cheers." Jake said as she handed him his glass.

"Again?"

"Yeah, this time to an incredible golf game and to an incredible golfer."

She raised her glass. "Ditto."

"And hopefully not the last game?" he asked after taking a sip.

She grinned coyly. "Hopefully not."

"Good. Everyone had a fun time. You fit right in," He smiled, holding her glare for a few seconds before his attention was brought back to the barbeque by a sizzling noise. "I think everything here is good to go. How's inside?"

"Ready."

They ate quietly for a few minutes before Jake put his fork down and broke the silence. "Madison, I'd like to explain what happened with Mike at The Leeky Canoe a few weeks ago."

"You don't have to."

"But I want to. I actually want to talk to you about this, and…that's never happened."

Her heart raced because she knew exactly what he meant. Madison put her fork down and leaned back. "Then I want to listen."

He smiled warmly. "Mike is the older brother of my ex-fiancé, Becca. We met when I was 19, dated for four years, and were engaged for one before I broke it off." Jake shifted on the floor and took a deep breath. "She'd turned into another person the last year we were together and had become a pathological liar, lying just about everything, even petty things. But the worst part was that she got into cocaine and heroin pretty heavily and lied about it. When I began to realize there was a much bigger problem than I initially thought I tried getting her help, but she turned nasty, and when I tried telling her family they didn't believe me. It took me awhile to realize the kind of life she was leading was not the kind of life I had initially signed up for with her, so I called it off. A couple of weeks later she lost her job and then she got kicked out of her apartment and ended up having to move back in with her parents and they, along with Mike, still blame me for it all."

"When did you break the engagement off?"

"About eight months ago, and that's when things went from bad to worse."

"What do you mean?"

"She started calling me relentlessly and when I didn't pick up, she always left nasty messages. She'd also always somehow figure out where I was if I was out, then show up and try to talk to me there."

"Did you think about getting a restraining order?"

"I should have in hindsight, but I have a few buddies in town that are police, and I think that they must have said something to her because she suddenly stopped. But then Mike started showing up and harassing me for her. When we all went to Leeky that was the first time, besides the crew breakfast a few weeks ago, that I'd been out. I don't know if you remember, but Merry said it was nice to see me and that's why. Because no one has really seen me outside of work unless they come by the house. I think I figured enough time had passed when we went to Leeky that things would have cooled off and been okay."

"When was the last time you spoke to Becca?" she asked tenderly seeing the hurt in his eyes.

"The real Becca, the sober Becca? Almost two years ago. But the last time I saw the new Becca, she was practically unrecognizable. It's terrible the effects those drugs can have on a person characteristically and physically over time."

"This might be too personal of a question and you obviously don't have to answer, but what if she got clean? What would that mean for you guys?"

Jake took a bite of his steak and thought for a moment before answering. "I honestly haven't thought about it because our history together is so tainted and her getting clean is such an unbelievable thought at this point."

Madison rested her hand on his. "I'm sorry, Jake."

"Thank you, but it's okay. I mean, it's been a long road, but I've learned a lot about myself and relationships and what I'm willing and not willing to put up with because of what happened with her. Lying and drugs being at the top of that list."

Madison swallowed hard and took a large sip of her wine. She felt his gaze on her and knew that if she looked at him right now, he would be able to see through her and all the lies she'd said up until this point. She wanted to tell Jake about Annie and everything else right then, but if she did it would feel like she was hijacking their intimate conversation with her own baggage and she didn't want to take away from how open Jake was being with her.

"Can I be honest with you for a second?" he asked.

"Isn't that what we're doing?" she said playfully.

"I don't know very much about you, and that's fine, but ever since you started at Middleton, there's been something about you that I've been drawn to. And I don't want to be presumptuous, but I think you might feel it too? If you don't, that's completely fine and I'm so sorry if this makes you uncomfortable, but I wanted you to know that before…".

"Before what?" she asked, breathlessly.

"Before I asked if I could kiss you?"

In an instant, all the butterflies in her stomach were jolted awake. Her hands and armpits instantly became clammy, and her mouth went dry.

"Would that be alright?" he asked.

"Yes," she whispered.

Jake leaned over the table and cupped her face with his right hand.

Once their lips met, the butterflies went away, and a calmness overtook her. Jake kissed tenderly yet passionately, as if it were the last kiss he would ever have. When he began to pull away, Madison grabbed his shirt and brought him back. To say it was the best kiss she'd ever had would be a gross understatement and Madison knew right then and there that that was what love was supposed to feel like.

Keeping their lips locked, Jake started to stand. He held her hands to help guide her from the coffee table as well. Once standing, he pulled her tight against his body. "There, that's better," he whispered. They stood kissing sensually for a few minutes before Madison began to lay back on the coach, leading him with her.

"Madison-"

"Let's just keep kissing." she said between their lips meeting.

They laid on the couch, so they were facing one another and holding each other's hands. His kisses were so captivating, and his lips were so soft that Madison felt like she was flying. Her heart was pounding so hard, but her mind felt at ease and she knew now that she could tell him everything because there was an undeniable connection between them.

At some point later in the evening, their kissing slowed, and they drifted to sleep on the couch. Madison woke the next morning to see their unfinished plates and half-empty wine glasses on the table next to them. She could feel Jake's strong arms wrapped around her and couldn't help but smile. It wasn't her plan to stay the night, but none of what had happened since she had moved to Meaford had been part of her plan.

Madison saw her cell phone on the floor a couple feet away and was curious of the time. Carefully, she pulled her arm away hoping not to wake Jake. It was light out, so she knew it was at least seven o'clock, but she wasn't sure when Scott or Jules planned on returning and didn't exactly like the idea of them walking in on her and Jake laying like they were.

"Good morning," he mumbled, squeezing her tightly and kissing the back of her head.

Her heart skipped a beat. "Good morning," she repeated forgetting about her phone and the time and turning over.

He pulled her in closer to him as he rolled onto his back. "Well, this sucks." She froze. "I'm pretty damn comfortable here with you and I want to kiss you again, but I have absolutely terrible morning breath and the only way to fix that would be for me to leave this comfy couch and brush my teeth."

She sighed in relief. "I think that's what they call a conundrum. But if it's any consolation, I'm comfortable too, also have terrible morning breath, and would like to kiss you again as well."

He turned his head to face Madison and grinned before kissing her. "What's your plan for the day? Will you stay for breakfast?"

"I think I could do that."

"Good. We're still on for lunch tomorrow too, right?"

She nodded.

"Can I make you a coffee or tea?"

"Coffee would be great, thank you."

Jake kissed her once more before sitting up and craning his neck. "I'd really like for this sleepover thing to happen again too, but maybe somewhere a little more comfortable next time. My body is sore like an old man's."

She laughed as she stretched and agreed. "We're not getting any younger, are we?"

Jake carried the dinner plates from the coffee table into the kitchen before turning the kettle on and scooping ground coffee into their French press.

Madison brought their wine glasses over and began to do the dishes.

Jake came up behind her. "No, no," he said wrapping his arms around her. "You don't need to do those, I'll do them later."

She turned around and as they were about to kiss again there was a knock on the front door.

"Jake?" a man called. "Scott?"

"Robert," Jake whispered. "He was one of the coastguards in the boat when we were by the lighthouse that morning," he explained, when he saw her confused expression.

Jake reluctantly let go of Madison and went to answer the door.

"Good morning, Robert."

"Hey man, sorry to knock so early, but as I was driving by to start my shift, I saw that the tire's on that car are slashed," he said, pointing to Madison's car parked on the road in front of Jake and Scott's house. "Do you know whose it is? It didn't look like Jules' car...."

"What?" Jake said in disbelief.

Upon hearing Jake's voice rise, Madison went to the door.

They followed Robert outside to Madison's car only to find that he had been right, both of her driver's side tires had been slashed. "Becca," he grumbled. "Or Mike. One of the Smiths'." He looked around as if whoever did it would still be there. He took Madison's hand. "I'm sorry. Let me call Scott's dad; he's a mechanic and can bring your car to his shop and fix this." He pulled out his cell phone and began dialing.

"Maybe I just ran over some glass or something?" Madison suggested but both him and Robert shook their heads.

"That's very kind of you to think of an alternative to someone purposefully doing it, but I'm sorry, this was deliberate, and I'm pretty sure I know who did it." He stepped away once Scott's dad began talking on the other line. After a few moments, he returned. "Scott's dad is on his way. He'll probably be able to fix your car today."

"Glad to hear that," Robert said. "Listen, I got to get to work, though."

"Yeah, of course, thank you, Robert."

"Thank you." Madison smiled.

"I'm really sorry, Madison. If insurance doesn't cover your tires, I'll pay for new ones."

"No, Jake-"

"Please," he said firmly. "This was definitely Becca or Mike and they're my problem. You shouldn't have to put up with their anger."

Madison replied reluctantly, "Okay."

"Thank you. How about we talk about something happier, like our lunch date tomorrow?"

She smirked. "So, tomorrow's a date now and not just two people sharing a meal?"

"If you're okay with it, I'd like everything to be a date from now on between us."

She smiled and nodded. "How about you come over and I make you lunch tomorrow?"

"You're inviting me over?"

Madison slowly nodded her head. "I am. You wowed me with your steaks and vegetable skewers, so let me wow you with something."

"You've already wowed me with something," he said kissing her.

"Jake, I need to tell you something. A few things actually, and I should have told you them sooner...."

But just as Madison was about to tell Jake everything, a tow truck appeared in front of them.

"Sorry, that's Scott's dad. Can it wait?" Jake asked waving to him.

She hesitated before responding. "...Yes."

After Madison's car had been towed to the mechanic's shop, Jake had insisted they call the police to file a report. It had taken a little persuading on Madison's part, but she had finally convinced him to leave the police out of it.

Scott's dad had the correct tires Madison's car needed as replacements and, thankfully, her insurance covered them. It didn't take long to exchange them and within an hour Madison was dropping Jake back off at home.

"Well, that wasn't how I planned the morning to go," he said when she'd parked in his driveway. "Do you want to come in for a coffee and something to eat?"

"I would, but I also think I should probably go home. I do have a date to prepare for you know!"

"You don't have to get too fancy on me or anything. I'd be content with mac n' cheese."

"Mac n' cheese is fancy." She teased.

"I had a really good time last night, Madison. Thank you for staying even though it wasn't the potluck we had planned."

"I had a good time, too. And I'm glad it wasn't the potluck we had planned."

Jake leaned across the console of her car and kissed her.

"There was something you wanted to tell me, wasn't there?" he asked pulling back.

Madison was about to answer when she saw Scott's truck pull up.

"Yeah, but it can wait until tomorrow."

Chapter Seven

Once leaving Jake's, Madison stopped at the grocery store to pick up what she would need for their lunch tomorrow. She really wanted to impress Jake, so she chose one of her family's favourite recipes: smoked salmon, cream cheese and purple onion with dill and parsley on a baguette.

For the first time in months, Madison found herself feeling very content and happy throughout the day and well into the evenings. However, despite that, she still found it difficult to sleep most nights. With the rain and cooler air having returned, Saturday evening was no exception. Annoyed that she was tossing and turning throughout the night, Madison decided her time could be better spent getting things prepared for her and Jake's lunch.

Turning the kettle on to make coffee, Madison pulled the ingredients out of the fridge and set them on the counter before getting to work. She turned the kitchen radio on and the classic 'I Can't Give You Anything but Love' by Louis Armstrong and Sy Oliver was playing. She hummed along as she began to scoop the baguette's insides out.

"There's just something about him, Annie," Madison said smiling in the empty cottage. "I tried to ignore Jake, but it was like no matter how hard I avoided him or was distant, something was always pulling me back. And he apparently feels the same way. He basically said that right before he asked to kiss me! He's just so…different. He's open and says how's he's feeling or what he's thinking, he's a gentleman, and he's nothing like Patrick." She took a cutting board out of a drawer and began chopping onions. "It might look like it's all happened quite quickly, well, I guess it kind of has. I mean, I just thought I'd go through the summer having a little crush on him, but the more time we spent together the more I fell for him and everything with Jake just feels right." Madison placed the chopped onions in a bowl and then added the cream cheese, fresh parsley and dill, mustard, olive oil, and salt and pepper to it.

"Oh, and his ex-sounds crazy! Like, legitimately. He's pretty sure she's the one that slashed my tires. Which is creepy because we were sleeping on the couch and the blinds were wide open! She easily could have peered through a window-"

The music on the radio stopped abruptly and turned to loud white noise. Madison jumped at the sound, dropping the spatula she was mixing ingredients with. Hurriedly she crossed the kitchen to turn it off. A few moments passed before Madison realized she was holding her breath.

She exhaled slowly. "Becca's crazy? Ha, says the girl that's talking to her dead best friend alone in a kitchen." Madison turned around and rested her hands on the countertop. Closing her eyes, she took several deep breaths, each one growing more and more aggravated. "What am I doing? Oh my god, Annie, I'm so sorry! I moved to Meaford to be invisible while trying to learn how to deal with losing you, not to fall for someone. I shouldn't have gone to Leeky or golfing, I shouldn't have stayed over, I shouldn't have kissed him, and I sure as hell shouldn't be bragging about him to you. I don't deserve this after what happened to you. This isn't right. None of this is right!" she shouted.

Grabbing the bowl of mixed ingredients, Madison threw it across the room. Connecting with the wall, the bowl dented its drywall and food splattered everywhere.

Uncontrollable tears ran down Madison's cheeks as she slid her way down the kitchen cupboards to the floor. She felt the anger and guilt she had suppressed over the last few days returning. Once again, the heaviness of Annie's death consumed her, and it felt like all the gains she thought she had made since moving to Meaford had evaporated. No matter how hard she tried to subdue what had happened in the accident, there was no other way of looking at it: Madison had killed her best friend and murderers didn't deserve kindness.

"What's that look for?" Jules asked seeing Jake's reaction to a text message. They sat around the breakfast buffet eating waffles with Scott.

"Madison texted me early this morning saying our lunch date is off."

"Really?" she asked surprised.

"Yeah."

"What does it say exactly?"

"'Can't do lunch. Sorry. See you tomorrow at work.'"

"That is strange." Jules agreed.

"This doesn't feel right." Jake offered.

"What do you mean?" Scott asked.

"I don't know how to explain it, but I think there's more to why she moved up here than she's letting on. Which would explain why when she had first started work, she was a bit standoffish or why she told us she didn't golf or want to make friends up here." He took another bite of waffle while his mind raced. "There was something she said she wanted to tell me yesterday, but the tow truck came right when she was about to tell me and then Scott pulled in the driveway when she tried to again. She said she would tell me today, though."

"Maybe she got cold feet?" Jules offered.

"What are you going to do?" Scott asked.

"I don't know. Her text wasn't inviting, so it doesn't sound like she wants me over there...."

"Maybe she just needs a friend but doesn't know it?" Jules suggested.

"What do you mean?"

"Well, if she moved up here because she's dealing with something that she's struggling with, maybe she's struggling because she's trying to figure it out on her own when really she needs help from a friend…."

Jake thought about what she said as he took a sip of coffee. "If she is dealing with something, I don't want to come on too strong."

Jules rested her hand on her brother's forearm. "Jake, you are the most genuine person I've ever met, you could never come on too strong. Besides, you're only hesitating because your spidey senses are going!"

"Spidey senses?" Scott and Jake questioned in unison.

"Yeah, ever since Becca."

"Madison's nothing like Becca. She wouldn't lie."

"I didn't mean that Madison was lying, I just meant that you always felt like there was something else going on with Becca, just like how you said you think there's more going on with Madison."

Jake wiped his mouth on a napkin before standing up. "I should go find out what's going on."

Madison was jolted awake by knocking on her front door.

"Madison?"

Jake. What was he doing here? She thought as she slowly got up from the cold kitchen floor. She must have cried herself to sleep right there on the ground after she had texted him saying she couldn't do lunch. She had texted him, right? She picked up her phone from the counter to double check she sent the text. She did. So, what was he doing here then?

"Madison?" He knocked again.

She could just pretend she wasn't home and hope he eventually went away.

"I know you're in there," he added softly.

Nope. She reluctantly stood up and went to the front door. Jake's features softened when he saw her. "Hey."

Standing with the door opened only slightly, she mumbled, "Didn't you get my text?"

"I did, but I wanted to make sure everything was alright."

"Everything's fine."

"Madison, I know that face," he said gently.

"What face?"

"The face you have right now. The 'I'm-trying-to-be-strong' face."

How the hell did he know that? "I don't know what you're talking about, but I just don't want to see you, okay?"

She regretted saying it as soon as the words slipped out of her mouth, but her cruelty didn't seem to faze him.

"I'm sorry, but I don't believe that. I'm not going home."

"What?" She snapped. "Well, you're not coming in."

"That's fine, I'll stay out here on the porch if I have to. We don't need to talk, but I think you need to be with someone that cares about you right now and that person's me."

"How do you know what I need, Jake? Go home."

Again, she regretted her words instantly. What had gotten into her? Why was she being so mean to him?

He took a step forward. "I'm sorry, but I'm not doing that. I can tell you're struggling with something, and you don't need to tell me what that is, but I think you need a friend so here I am."

Part of her wanted to keep fighting Jake, but in her heart, she knew he was right. Leaving the front door open, she turned around and walked back inside.

Jake tentatively followed her but stopped when he saw the bowl of food she had thrown earlier. Within seconds, he walked into the kitchen and opened the cupboards under the sink.

Pulling out a spray bottle of cleaner, he grabbed paper towel from the counter and began cleaning up the food.

"Jake, what are you doing? You didn't come over here to do that. Stop."

Jake ignored her and continued cleaning.

"'Stop!' I said!" Madison shouted.

Jake stopped and slowly stood up.

"I'm sorry," she whispered, embarrassed.

He walked to the garbage bin and put the dirty paper towel in. "I would just like to keep you company if that's okay. We don't need to talk or even be in the same room, but I'd just like to be here for you."

"Why are you being so nice to me?"

"Because that's what friends do."

Madison wasn't in the right frame of mind to get too hung up on his use of the word 'friends'. She took a deep breath. "Look, I'm sorry you came all this way, but I have nothing for lunch now," she said.

He stuck his index finger up, motioning for her to wait a moment. He left the cottage and went to his car. When he returned, he had an arm behind his back. "That's okay, because I have something that we could eat for lunch." Smirking, he revealed a box of macaroni n' cheese. "Or breakfast if you haven't eaten yet?"

She couldn't help but give a soft smile at the sight of the box and shook her head.

Jake took her smile as confirmation that he could make her mac n' cheese. As he moved his way around her kitchen, Madison began to feel foolish.

"Jake, I can do-"

"No, let me do this. Forget that I'm here and I'll bring this to you when it's ready."

Madison didn't want to argue with him again, so she conceded, grabbing a blanket from the couch and went out the back door. Wrapping herself in it, she sat in her usual chair and watched the rain beat down on the waters of Georgian Bay.

It wasn't long before Jake brought her out a bowl of macaroni n' cheese and sat in the chair opposite her. They sat in silence as she devoured the bowl. She hadn't realized how hungry she had been and was thankful, in more ways than one, that Jake was sitting there with her. Unlike most people's approach, he wasn't hounding her for answers or hovering over her to see if she was alright or wanted to talk. Which was something she didn't expect but saw now that it was exactly what she needed.

"There's something I want to tell you," she said staring at the lake.

From her peripheral vision, she could see Jake turn his body, so he was facing her.

"I killed my best friend," she said bluntly as a tear gently rolled down her cheek. "She was at a party where she drank too much, so she called me to pick her up. She'd actually asked me to go with her, but I didn't feel like it and thought, 'I'll just go to the next party.' We were less than a block away from her house and a truck ran a red light." Madison wiped her cheek with the back of her right hand. "I know I wasn't driving the truck, but I should have looked both ways in the intersection, and I should have just gone to that stupid party because then I wouldn't have been driving and Annie would still be alive."

The tears came uncontrollably then and within one swift movement, Jake was kneeling in front of her. "Come here," he whispered hugging her.

"Everyone kept saying that it wasn't my fault, but I could see it in their eyes that they didn't mean it. *I* was driving, *I* was the sober one! *I* should have known to look both ways!" she cried.

Jake gently rubbed her back. "I know you feel guilty and that you feel like her death is your fault, and it's okay to *feel* that, but not to *live* by that, Madison. I know our friendship and relationship are still new, but from what I know about you I feel like the person that you would have chosen to be your best friend also wouldn't want you to live with this guilt."

Madison pulled back and wiped her cheeks again with the blanket. "How can you feel guilty and not live by that guilt?"

He frowned. "Practice."

"That sounds like something that's a lot easier said than done." She slowly shook her head. "You know, I moved up here to get away from everyone and everything that kept reminding me of Annie. The plan was to just keep to myself and grieve alone which is why I was so reluctant about hanging out when I first started at Middleton. I thought I'd be the only young person and so it'd be easy to keep to myself, but it turns out everyone working there is close to my age and you were all so nice to me…. I started having fun again and that's not fair because none of this would be happening if I didn't kill Annie. *We* would never have met! Friday night would never have happened and that's not fair." Madison sobbed into Jake's shoulder again and he pulled her in tightly.

"I'm so sorry, Madison. But that's what I mean. I bet Annie wouldn't want you to be putting your life on hold because you think it's what you deserve for the accident." He held her while she cried. It wasn't until her crying slowed that he continued. "When you answered the door…you had the same expression I had after I lost my mom, which is why I was so insistent that I stay. I remember that face and those feelings of just needing to feel someone in the house with you. No forced talking, just someone's presence was enough to make me feel not so alone. I mean, my dad and Jules were there but we were all grieving in our own way."

Madison pulled back from him. "Does it get better?"

"It gets…different. Mothers and best friends are irreplaceable. Thank you for telling me about Annie. I know you're going to think whatever you want about what happened, but please remember that while your feelings are valid and important, you can't shape what happens in your life around the accident. You were doing the right thing and being responsible by picking Annie up, the truck driver did the wrong thing by running a red light and because of that he created an accident that killed Annie. How were you after the accident? Were you hurt?"

Madison nodded. "But I just had some cuts and bruises and had to stay for a day so they could monitor my vitals."

"I wish I knew you then so I could have been there for you. Is there anything I can do now to help make you feel better?"

She gave an appreciative smile. "No, you being here is great and finally telling you feels really good. I wanted to tell you a few times before, but it never felt like the right time."

"Was that what you wanted to tell me yesterday morning?"

"Yeah." While that was partially true, Madison felt drained and didn't want to get into her job history or job potential in the golf course industry with him right now.

"You look exhausted, Madison."

"I didn't sleep very well last night. Can we just sit out here together for a little while longer, please?"

"Of course." Jake squeezed her hand a couple times before getting up and sitting back in the chair across from her.

Madison wasn't sure when she drifted off, but when she awoke, she was in her bedroom with the blanket she had out on the porch draped over her. *How did I get here?* Madison walked out of her bedroom to find the kitchen, living room and verandah empty.

"Jake?" she called walking towards the front to see if his truck was still in the driveway. It wasn't.

Entering the kitchen, she noticed that he had cleaned the dishes from the macaroni n' cheese, but also the dishes she used to start making what would have been their lunch.

Wanting to call to say thank you and to apologize, she headed back to the bedroom to get her phone. While on her way, something caught her eye and she stopped.

Where the bowl had indented the wall, it had been fixed and there was a note taped next to it:

I didn't want to wake you or leave you outside, but I had to get going because I have a conference in London for the week that Scott and I need to attend. We're leaving tonight because it starts at 8:00 AM tomorrow morning (sorry, I was going to tell you today about it). I'll be back Thursday night and will see you at work Friday morning. Please text or call me if you need anything. For the wall: Let dry for 24hrs, sand, wipe clean, then repaint.

Jake x

Chapter Eight

Madison wouldn't say that she was counting down the days until Jake was back from his conference, but she was excited. Work that week had felt weird while he was away, even though they rarely worked together and could even go most of the day without seeing one another, she liked knowing that he was close by. Since her second day at Middleton Golf Course, Madison had continued to arrive earlier than everyone else in the mornings to help Jake prepare the machines and tools for the day. Because Madison was an extra set of hands, they had fallen into an easy pattern of who did what based on what jobs people were going to be doing. At first, Madison started joining him because she couldn't sleep, but as the weeks went on, she found herself looking forward to that time spent together.

Madison had offered to help Jules and Evelyn get things ready for Drew's pre-bachelor party barbeque that they were having at the maintenance shop Friday afternoon. Thankfully, this helped keep her mind on something other than Jake. Madison had wanted to text him many times throughout the week, but she refrained. Even though there were many things she wanted to say, she understood that he was away for work and didn't want to overload him with messages. She'd expressed gratitude for his kindness and apologized again for her behaviour, but she also knew she needed to apologize again in person once he was back.

Madison had spent a lot of time that week thinking about how she acted Sunday morning and problem-solving how to handle her emotions the next time something like that happened. Although they were beginning to get fewer and farer between, she knew it was only a matter of time before the grief and guilt of Annie's death would overcome her once again and she didn't want to behave like she had.

Madison wanted to not only say she was sorry, but also do something sweet for him to show that she was sorry too. She had a few ideas but would need help from Jules to keep it a surprise for when he came home.

"So, Drew's work barbeque is Friday and then his bachelor party starts right afterwards for the weekend?" Madison asked Jules in the lunchroom while they were on break.

Jules poured herself some more coffee. "Yeah. He was actually supposed to be at the conference the guys are at solo, but he made a trade with them that if they went in his place, he would cover a couple weekend shifts of theirs."

"How come?"

"He figured being away all week and then being away for his bachelor party that same weekend - a week before his wedding - wasn't the greatest idea."

"That was probably a smart move," Madison laughed.

"Totally. And of course, Jake and Scott said they'd just go to the conference for him and that Drew didn't need to cover any of their shifts, but he's insistent on being fair."

"That's good. Are Drew and Evelyn going on a honeymoon?"

"Yeah, but in the winter. He can't exactly take time off in the summer and Evelyn's totally cool with that. Being home in the summer is her favourite time of year anyway."

"Where are they going?"

"Antarctica!" Jules said excitedly as she finished her coffee.

"What?" Madison exclaimed.

"And hiking through Patagonia on their way down!"

"That's amazing."

"No kidding! Their reasoning is that they won't be able to do another big trip like it once they have kids – well, at least for a while anyways."

"That's really cool."

"Right?" Jules leaned back against the counter. "So, are you going to come to their wedding next weekend?"

Madison hesitated.

"Look, I don't know what happened Sunday between you and Jake, and I don't need to know, but I do know that he likes you. And I know I'm biased because he's my brother, but he's a really good guy and was going through a bout of bad luck until you moved here. Plus, he needs a dancing partner, and he's really good at dancing. But don't tell him I told you that!"

Madison smiled. "I would like to go. But I was hoping you could help me with something first…."

Thursday evening finally arrived, and using Jules's help, Madison was able to make sure that Jake dropped Scott off at her place before he made his way home from the conference.

Madison took a few deep breaths as she eagerly awaited Jules's text saying that Jake was on his way. For her surprise, Madison had decided to recreate the lunch date that they were supposed to have last Sunday for Jake for when he got home. While it was almost nine o'clock, she still made the same smoked salmon, cream cheese and purple onion on a baguette for them. Additionally, she made crème brûlée for dessert, got a bottle of Jake's favourite red wine, and had her iTunes ready to play his favourite music – courtesy of Jules's intel.

When she finally received the text, Madison knew she had less than 10 minutes before Jake would arrive. She hit play on her phone and the Australian tropical house DJ, Thomas Jack, filled the room.

Her car was parked on the street in front of Jake's house, so she knew that as soon as he pulled onto his road, he would know that she was there and that something was going on.

Within minutes she heard his truck pull into the driveway. She took one final deep breath and gave her armpits one last smell check.

With the front door open, Jake would be able to hear Thomas Jack playing through the screen door and see the candles that were lit in the front foyer.

"What...is...this?" She heard him say to himself as he unlatched the screen door.

Upon seeing Madison, he smiled and dropped his bag. "Hey you." He hugged her tightly and breathed deeply into her shoulder. "Well, this is an awesome surprise. Now I get why you were so flippant with my text messages earlier; you had something up your sleeve!"

She raised her eyebrows and gave him a 'you-caught-me-face'. "I know it's late and that you must be exhausted from your week and the drive back, so if this is too much, I totally get it. But I feel terrible for how I treated you and for how I spoke to you Sunday. I wasn't in the right frame of mind and you deserve better than that. Thank you for being so kind and fixing the wall, making lunch, doing the dishes, and just being there for me. I know I wasn't the easiest person to be around and, again, I'm sorry for that."

He cupped her face with his hands. "You're welcome."

"So, I wanted to recreate the lunch date we were supposed to have Sunday afternoon, tonight!" She stepped aside for him to see his buffet counter set-up with their food and drink.

"Is that crème brûlée and Silk & Spice red wine? Wait, and is Thomas Jack playing? What's going on?"

"I did some investigative work about some of your favourite things while you were away," Madison winked. "How are you feeling, though? I know it's getting late." Madison checked her watch and saw that it was now 9:30 PM.

Jake smiled. "I'm feeling great now and I'm starving, so this is perfect."

She returned his smile. "Good. Well, dig in and tell me all about the conference."

Jake began telling her about his week and the various keynote speakers and educational lectures that him and Scott attended. Because they were there in Drew's place, they kept detailed notes throughout each session so they could have a thorough debrief with Drew Monday morning.

"Which lecture was your favourite?"

"There were a couple that I ended up liking more than I thought I would. One was about 'How Golf Became Cool Again' and another was 'How to Use Social Media Strategically for Your Golf Club."

"Oh yeah? And how *did* golf become cool again or how *can* you use social media strategically?" she asked taking a sip of wine. She put her glass down when she caught him staring. "What?"

Jake shook his head.

"What?" she insisted.

"Nothing, it's just…." He tapped the buffet table with his fingers, clearly nervous. "I knew I had a good feeling about you and I'm glad that I was right. This, right now, feels easy. I mean, I'm also glad we've already talked about the hard stuff: my mom, Becca, and Annie. I know we didn't really talk about my mom, and we will, but you know that she died and if you didn't it would have just felt like an elephant in the room for me." He rested his hand on hers. "Thank you for tonight."

"Sorry if it feels rushed, but I didn't know when we would get a moment alone together with the barbeque tomorrow and bachelor party over the weekend. And, selfishly, I wanted to see you."

"Well, I'm glad you did because I wasn't sure when we'd get a moment either, which is part of why you doing this is so great. To be honest, when I hadn't heard back from you today,

I was considering popping over tonight anyways; just to see you and check in."

"Well, that would have been very sweet, but I couldn't text you back without giving something about tonight away. But wait, there's actually a second part to this date."

Jake turned on the bar stool he was sitting on so that he was completely facing her. "Oh?"

"I was wondering if you would like to be my date to Drew and Evelyn's wedding?"

Jake perked up. "For real? Of course!" He kissed her cheek. "I'm so happy you decided to come! You should know that I'm a dancing machine at weddings, though. Unstoppable one might say."

"Oh, I've got moves, too." Madison replied winking.

"You should also know that my dad will be there. I hope meeting him so soon won't be too weird?"

She shook her head. "I look forward to meeting your dad."

"Good. He's looking forward to meeting you too."

Madison was surprised. "He knows about me?"

"Of course, he does. Now, tell me about your week."

They talked for a little while longer before Madison went home. Jake had offered Madison to stay over, but she politely declined. While part of her really wanted to spend the night at Jake's, she didn't want to rush things any faster than they were already going.

Work Friday morning went by slower than Madison expected it to. Even though her and Jake had planned to meet earlier and set equipment up like they normally did, there was an irrigation leak that had him out on the course by the time Madison had arrived at Middleton. While it was nice having

Jake back, she was sad it wouldn't be until lunch that she saw him again.

Madison spent the morning leapfrogging cutting tees with Robbie before work officially ended for the day around 11:00 AM. The festivities and barbeque weren't supposed to start for another hour, but there were things that needed to get done around the shop to prepare.

On the chalkboard in the lunchroom, Jules had written a list of jobs that needed to be done and spread them amongst everyone. Madison's was to help Jules put the decorations up around the lunchroom as well as outside where they'd be eating.

For barbeques, Ben and Drew brought theirs strapped in the beds of their trucks in the morning. Having two barbeques would allow Jake and Ben, whose jobs were the official barbequers, to cook everything at once so everyone could eat at the same time. Scott and Oskar had picked up picnic tables from a nearby park, so there was somewhere for everyone to sit. The picnic tables' tops were covered with a variety of salads Jules, Evelyn, and Evelyn's mom had made, bowls of chips, and some cookies and brownies that Madison had baked.

With things almost ready, Madison was inside the lunchroom taping one of the final streamers up when Jake walked in.

"Hey you", he smiled, kissing her cheek. "It looks great in here and outside. Drew's going to love it. Is there anything I can do to help?"

"Oh no you don't! Don't think you can deviate from Jules's list! You're supposed to be barbequing," she said stepping down from the chair and pointing to the board where his and Ben's names were next to 'Barbeque'.

"I know, I know, but I wanted to sneak a minute in here alone with you so I could ask what you're up to Sunday?"

"Hanging out with you?"

Jake stepped closer to her. "I was hoping you would say that. I'm not sure what the plan is for Sunday with the bachelor party or when things will end, but probably after lunch sometime. Can I text you over the weekend when I have a better idea?"

"Of course. Take your time on Sunday, though. No rush, I'll be around."

He took another step closer and put his hands on her waist. "Good."

"Jake! The barbeques have heated up and are ready to go!" Ben called inside the shop's door.

"Duty calls." He took her hands into his and gave them a quick squeeze before heading out of the lunchroom.

Even at Jake's slightest touch, the butterflies in her stomach began doing backflips. She took a deep breath and shook the smile off her face. As she climbed back on the chair to finish putting the streamers up, Robbie burst through the shop door.

"Madison, do you want to throw a football around?" he asked tossing her one just as she turned around. "Nice reflexes!" he said when she caught it. "I bet you can throw, too!"

Madison taped the remaining streamer up and tossed the ball back to him. "I can throw a spiral," she said shrugging her shoulders. "Where's Jules, though? Are all of the jobs done?"

Robbie nodded. "We're just waiting for Drew to come now."

"Then, yes, I do want to throw a football around," she said smiling, knowing Robbie was in for a surprise.

What no one at Middleton knew was that Madison had grown up learning how to play football with Annie's older brothers. When Annie and Madison were little, her brothers wouldn't let them play football with them – or even catch – because they were girls. So, Madison and Annie practiced relentlessly until they were just as good, if not better, as her brothers. Then, her brothers always wanted Madison and Annie on their team or playing catch with them.

"Do you want to play 'Donkey'?" Robbie asked throwing her the ball when she was several feet away.

"Sure," she replied throwing it back in a perfect spiral, but Robbie fumbled the ball.

"Do you know how the game works?" he asked picking it up.

"Yeah, and you have a 'D'" Madison smiled innocently.

While Robbie and Madison continued their game, Jake and Ben barbequed, and everyone else from the maintenance shop began taking seats around the picnic tables.

Since it was the end of the workday for people, and Drew's upcoming nuptial celebration, Ben and his wife bought beer for everyone to enjoy. The sun was shining, the day was getting warmer, and people were laughing while sipping on their cold beers. Despite Madison and Robbie playing catch, she couldn't help but notice the unusual sight in front of her: all her coworkers genuinely getting along and enjoying each other's company. Ruby Lewis's maintenance shop's comradery was fine, but this was different. Sure, some drinks were going around, but this was just another thing that made her feel like she might not want to leave Meaford at the end of the season anymore.

Drew was the last to arrive to his barbeque because he wanted to make sure that everything was prepared for the upcoming weekend when he, Jake, and Scott would be away, and he wanted things to run smoothly. When he finally did arrive, everyone stood up clapping.

"Food's ready!" Ben called a few minutes later.

Everyone quickly gathered around the barbeques with paper plates and a hamburger or a sausage bun. Once people had taken some salad and grabbed a seat again at the picnic tables, Ben stood up holding his beer.

"I don't want to give away any spoilers from my speech next weekend, but I would like to say a few things. Drew, from the moment Evelyn brought her new 'friend' home after school when you were in grade two, I have always liked you. And that's hard for a father to say when his little girl, at seven years old, says she has a boyfriend. But you've always been a respectable young man, so it was hard not to like you. And trust me, I tried - especially during the teen years," Ben laughed, and everyone else joined in. "I've watched you grow up parallel to Evelyn and seen the two of you go through the various stages of being kids, teenagers, young adults, and now grown-ups. Yet, through all those different times, you were always there for our daughter, which made her mother, Kate, and I very happy. But for the last four years, I've been able to see you in a different light and separate from Evelyn: as my boss. And I'll be honest, I didn't think I could respect you any more than I already did, but I do. You are a compassionate, reasonable, smart, responsible, and an invaluable boss, and I couldn't be happier not only to work for you but to have you finally officially joining our family. You've always been my son, but next weekend it's just going to be legal. Could everyone please raise their drinks? To our boss and my future son-in-law, Drew."

"To Drew!" everyone repeated, clinking their beers.

Drew stood up and gave Ben a big hug. "Thank you, Ben, and thank you to everyone else for helping put this together. Also, for picking up any slack while two very valuable employees were away this week at a conference in my place, and for this weekend while I'm having my bachelor party. I couldn't be happier to be marrying my best friend, to have incredible in-laws, and to have such an exceptional crew of employees. Life just keeps getting better and better." He raised his beer again. "To you guys, thank you."

Once again, everyone joyfully clinked their drinks. People resumed eating their food and chatting for another couple of hours. Time slipped by quickly playing a few more games of catch with the football and a few rounds of Euchre with cards someone had brought.

With the beer flowing, by the time Evelyn pulled up in her mother's van, everyone was feeling pretty good. She got out and hugged Jules who was standing next to Robbie at the end of the picnic table.

"Okay, so besides Robbie, who else has had too much to drink that I'm driving home?" she asked patting him on the back.

"Whys you just assumes that I've had too much?" Robbie sputtered, hiccupping.

"Exactly." She laughed. "You can just grab a seat in the back, but make sure you have a bag or bowl or something with you."

"I would love a ride," Jules said.

"You got it, girl! How did the barbeque go?"

"It was really great, but I'm pretty sure your dad's gotten Drew drunk already."

"So, he's going to need a barf bag for the limo that Connor's picking them up in. Where is Drew?" she asked looking around.

"He's in his office with your dad and Scott."

"Uh oh, that could only mean that the scotch has been brought out," she said smiling and walking towards the maintenance shop door.

Upon walking into Drew's office, Evelyn found him, her father, and Scott sitting around his desk with a bottle of scotch between them.

Drew beamed from his chair when he saw Evelyn but practically took her out as he tried to stand and greet her.

"Dad, are you getting my almost husband wasted before his bachelor party even starts?"

"Yes, yes I am," Ben retorted proudly.

"Well, don't mind me, I'm just collecting anyone that's not going tonight and driving them home," Evelyn said kissing

Drew and hugging her dad. "Have a great time over the weekend, guys!" she said waving as she left Drew's office.

Back outside at the picnic table with Jules and Robbie now sat Madison, Jake, and Oskar.

"Hey Madison, would you like a drive home?" Evelyn asked. "I'm taking everyone home that needs a ride."

"No, thank you. I'm close enough that I can walk."

"Oskar, can you handle Robbie in the back of the van? Jules and I will be up front."

"You got it!" he said, slinging Robbie's left arm around his neck and helping him walk to the van.

"Have a fun weekend, Jake!" Evelyn and Jules said in unison while waving goodbye to Madison.

Once the van pulled away, Jake and Madison were left alone at the picnic table.

"I should probably get going, too. It sounds like you're going to have quite the weekend," she said smiling as she stood up.

Jake also stood and followed behind her as she walked to the edge of the maintenance shop that faced the road leading to her cottage. "It will be a great time for sure," he agreed. "But I kind of want it to be Sunday already."

Madison took his hands in hers. "Me too. But make sure you have fun! I'll see you Sunday." She kissed his cheek and turned to leave, but Jake didn't let go of her hands and before she knew it, she was being pulled into his arms and being passionately kissed. The kiss was heated and all-encompassing and Madison's heart felt like it was beating a million miles a minute.

"I'll see you Sunday," Jake said pulling away as quickly as he had pulled her into him. He walked through the side maintenance shop door, but before the door closed, he turned smirking and winked.

Madison bit her lip as she backed away slowly from the maintenance shop and headed home; finally accepting the fact that she had in fact fallen head over heels for Jake.

Chapter Nine

Aside from working Saturday and Sunday morning, Madison had spent the weekend doing things around the house: giving the inside a good clean and tidying the yard. She had also called her parents and talked to them for a few hours Saturday night. She was more honest with them this time about how things were going for her in Meaford, how kind and welcoming her co-workers had been, and who she was spending time with. Her parents were relieved to hear that she was dealing with Annie's passing in more productive ways than she had been before, and that someone in Meaford knew about the struggles she was having over her best friend's death.

From Jake's late-night texts, it sounded like he was having a good time at Drew's bachelor party. When he wasn't telling her about the shenanigans they were up to, he was confessing his feelings for her, making it very apparent that he had fallen hard for Madison, too. Which she couldn't help but feel giddy about.

Like Jake had initially thought, after a final brunch with Drew and his buddies, that was the end of the bachelor party weekend. Connor, Drew's best man, had gone above and beyond for the entire weekend, and even had the limo that picked them up from the shop at Middleton Friday, drop each of them off at their homes on Sunday.

Jake called Madison just as the limo was pulling up to his and Scott's house. "I'd still love to hang out, but I'm going to need a couple hours of sleep and a cold shower before being presentable enough."

Madison laughed. "That works for me. It'll give me time to finish things up around here. How does a Bruce Trail hike sound? I can pick you up mid-afternoon?"

"That sounds perfect."

After they hung up, Madison finished working on the section of garden she had started earlier in the day before showering. Madison changed into hiking capris and a light-weight long-sleeved shirt and vest. While it was summer, there was a cool breeze blowing off the water and with the hottest part of the day already gone, she wanted to be prepared in case the day cooled off even more.

When she arrived at Jake and Scott's house, their front door was open and, upon Madison knocking on the screen door, she heard Scott's voice welcome her inside.

"Jake's just getting changed." He offered, when Madison entered their kitchen. Scott stood against the island counter with a bottle of aspirin and Gatorade next to him.

"How was the bachelor party?" Madison asked.

Scott took a deep breath. "A lot of fun, but we're all hurting today. I don't think many of us will be drinking again until the wedding Saturday."

"So, Jake won't be partaking in the beers I brought for our hike?"

Scott let out a long sigh. "Maybe. Jake has a bizarre ability to not get hangovers as badly as the rest of us."

"He's a hangover magician? What a jerk," She teased.

"Hey, sorry, I wasn't ready." Jake said, coming out of his bedroom and kissing her cheek. "Are you coming to dinner tonight at our dad's?" he asked Scott as he filled a water bottle in their kitchen sink.

"Even with this hangover, I wouldn't miss an invite to have dinner with your dad," Scott said.

Jake patted Scott on the shoulder. "I wish I could sympathize with your hangover, but feel better, man!"

As they walked out of his front door to Madison's car Jake slid his fingers into hers. "Every Sunday Jules and I go to our dad's for dinner. It's kind of been a tradition to go to his place Sunday's since Jules and I moved out of the house. Scott comes every now and then, too. Last week I couldn't go because of the conference, so it's important that I go tonight." He opened her driver's side door, and once Madison had fastened her seatbelt, gently closed it. He trotted around to the passenger door before continuing. "I'd really like for our date to not have to end after our hike today, so would you like to come to dinner at my dad's tonight? With Scott there, meeting my dad might not be as intense or awkward? Not that I think it would be intense or awkward, but you might think it would be?" He was floundering with his words and Madison couldn't help but think it was adorable.

She touched his hand and gave him a warm smile. "I would love to join you for dinner with your dad tonight. I think it's really sweet that it's a tradition of yours to have dinner with him weekly. We'll just have to drop by my place so I can change into dinner appropriate attire before we go over."

Jake kissed her cheek. "You don't need to change, you look great. Plus, my dad is a big hiker and knows we're hiking beforehand, so he won't be surprised to see us dressed like this." he said referring to his own hiking shorts and long sleeve shirt.

Madison hesitated. "Does he drink?" Jake nodded. "Well, then I'll at least bring him wine. Does he like red or white?"

Jake's features softened. "You don't need to do that either. Honestly, he just wants to meet you."

Madison raised her eyebrows waiting for an answer, but Jake wasn't budging. She squinted her eyes and stuck out her tongue before continuing. "Both kinds of wine it is then! We should go to the liquor store now before it closes and then we can go for our hike?"

"If you insist."

"I do. But before that, I have something for you." She reached behind her seat and presented Jake with a small bag.

"What is this?" he said more to himself than to her as he took it into his hands.

"Something that I'm not sure you'll need any more if what Scott said is true.... Open it."

Jake gave her a quizzical look before lifting the bag up and down in his hands. "Hm, well there's something in it that's slightly heavy, and it sounds almost like there's something liquidy inside, too." Pulling the tissue paper off the top of the gift bag, Jake saw a bottle of Gatorade. "Delicious flavour choice," he said noting that it was blue raspberry. He dug dipper into the bag and pulled out a small package of Advil and a McDonalds gift card.

"It's a hangover kit," Madison proudly announced. "But inside Scott said you don't get hangovers too badly, so it might not be as needed as I assumed it would after a bachelor party weekend."

"Gatorade to rehydrate, Advil for the headache and a McDonalds gift card for greasy food to absorb the alcohol in my system? This is so thoughtful! Thank you, Madison." Jake leaned across his seat and kissed her again. "I might not get hangovers as badly as most people, but every little bit helps. And this," he said lifting up the hangover kit's contents, "is helpful."

When they were inside the liquor store, Madison couldn't help but stare at Jake as he perused in a different aisle. She had an overwhelming sensation that everything they did together was destined to be. She knew that that was impossible, and Madison would give anything to have Annie back, but she felt like that in some divine way, Annie had made sure Madison and Jake met. Everything they did felt normal, and when they were together it felt like they had known each other for years even though they had only met a couple months ago. Not to mention that it was only recently that they started to become more than friends, and now she was picking what wine to bring when meeting his dad. But it all felt right, and Madison marveled in it while quietly thanking Annie.

Jake continued to insist that Madison didn't need to bring wine, so he gave no hints as to what kind his dad liked. However, despite that, Madison knew she couldn't show up to dinner empty handed and so she picked out her parents' favourite bottles of red and white wine to bring.

As they drove to where they would begin their hike, the weather began to get better. The cool breeze seemed to have gone away, as did any clouds that had previously been in the sky.

Once the car was parked and Madison grabbed her hydra pack from the backseat, they walked over to the trail map. They decided to only do a 5-kilometer loop so they could be on time for dinner at Jake's dads.

"After you," She smiled, extending her arm so Jake could take the lead. "So, Scott and your dad must get along well from his comment earlier about not missing an invite to have dinner with him?"

"Oh yeah, they always have. I mean, he's my best friend and I've known him for almost my entire life, so he's always just been around. To be honest, I think my dad actually started to like him even more once him and Jules started dating. It sounds odd, but Scott asked my dad if he could date Jules which, obviously, my dad loved because it's so old school."

"What? Really?"

"Yeah, he didn't bother asking me, mind you, but he asked my dad and my dad really appreciated it. Not that if he'd said Scott couldn't date Jules that would have stopped them, but my dad was impressed nonetheless."

"Were you angry that they hid it from you? Sorry, Jules mentioned that they dated in secret for a while when I first started work. I don't mean to throw her under the bus, it just came up because I thought *you* guys were dating!"

Jake scoffed. "Really?"

She blushed. "Yeah, I don't know what I was thinking."

"That would have really thrown a wrench in us getting together." Jake joked. "But yes and no. I understand why they would want to keep it a secret and not make their relationship bigger than it was before they even knew what it was. Plus, there was a lot going on with Becca at the time, so I can see why they would be apprehensive about telling me. But at the same time, I feel like they could have trusted me with it. I think I'm a pretty level-headed person and am not the kind of guy to try and tell my sister and best friend who they can or cannot date."

As the trail widened, Madison walked up beside him and took his hand in hers. "You are a very understanding friend and brother."

Jake laughed. "I don't know if Jules and Scott would agree wholeheartedly with you on that one, and I'm sure you're going to get stories tonight at dinner that will make you think otherwise."

"Doubtful, but I'm looking forward to hearing them just the same!"

As they continued along the trail, it brought them to many beautiful spots that overlooked the Beaver Valley, and at each one, they took a few moments to marvel at the natural beauty. Slowly but surely, they were making their way to the top of a small hill where Jake assured her had the most spectacular lookout.

"Do you trust me?" he asked as they neared the top.

Madison looked at him skeptically. "Yes?"

"Close your eyes then," he said taking her hand in his. "I'll let you know if you need to lift your feet higher or if there are rocks or roots." He slowly led Madison the last twenty feet before the trail and hill plateaued. Once there, he positioned

Madison at the perfect angle so she would have the best view. "Okay, open your eyes."

Madison slowly opened them and was awestruck by the rolling hills, the immense greenery, and how, from where she stood, it had the most picturesque view over the entirety of the valley.

"Wow, you weren't kidding. What a sight!"

"It is," he agreed, staring at her.

"How do you feel about taking a break and having a beer? Do we have time?" she asked taking her hydra pack off and sitting on a tree stump that was close by, facing the clearing.

"I think we do, and I would love one."

She took two Sidelaunch tall boys out of her pack and passed one to him.

"Cheers," they said in unison.

"You know, I have to admit, it's a bit strange and surreal that you chose this spot for us to do of all of the hikes around. And that, more specifically, we chose this trail and loop." Jake said, taking another sip of beer.

"How come?"

"Because this is where my dad proposed to my mom."

Madison almost spit the beer out of her mouth. "What? Really?" She wiped her mouth as she regained her composure. "Well, this is a very beautiful spot. Your dad must be a romantic."

"He is, and, like I said earlier, a hiker. They both were. This hike was also one of their first dates too, so this spot has a lot of significance with the Andrews clan."

"Is that why he chose to propose to her here?"

Jake nodded.

"Wow. That's so sweet. Did your parents do a lot of hiking?"

"Tons, and all over the world. But this hike and view was always their favourite. It's not much of a hike compared to the ones they'd done elsewhere, but I think because it had so much history for them and their relationship that's why it was their favourite."

"How did they meet?"

"High school. But they didn't start dating until the summer after first year university."

"Tell me about your mom," Madison said gently.

Jake took a deep breath. "She was the best. She was kind, patient, loving, loved to cook and dance and made Jules and I do both with her. Athletic, adventurous…. Name any good quality, and my mom had it."

"She sounds lovely. I wish I could have met her."

"Me too. But you'll be meeting the next best thing tonight: my dad."

"Has your dad dated anyone else since?"

"No, and he won't. Jules and I keep trying to get him to go out and meet women, but he won't hear any of it. Even though he knows our mom would have wanted him to, too."

"That's hard, but I get it. His love with your mom was once in a lifetime; a love to last."

Jake gave a weak smile and squeezed her hand. "Thanks. How are you doing, though?"

"I'm great," she replied leaning into him and taking another sip of beer.

He leaned into her as well and kissed the top of her head. "You know what I mean. How are you dealing with Annie since what happened last week?"

Madison took a deep breath. "Honestly? Better. I didn't think it was possible, but my nightmares have almost completely gone away, and my moments alone have become more constructive rather than destructive."

"That's great to hear. I'm sure Annie would be really proud of you."

"Thank you."

They sat quietly with one another, taking in the beautiful view and listening to the wildlife around them for a while. If anything, it was the most comfortable silence Madison had ever sat through, and before she knew it, they were done their beers, the sun was starting to dip in the sky, and they needed to start making their way back to Madison's car.

Jake stood and held his arms out so he could help Madison stand. She took his hands and he pulled her into his arms. "Thank you for this hike and thank you in advance for coming to dinner tonight."

She could feel her cheeks growing warm from the way he was staring at her. "Of course, Jake. But I really should be the one thanking you. You've made everything about me moving here better; you make me better."

He cupped her face in his hands and kissed her sensually. The butterflies in her stomach that had been at bay began doing backflips because it was then that Madison realized she was in love with Jake Andrews.

They made it to Jake's dad's in perfect time and just as Jules and Scott were simultaneously pulling into his driveway, too.

"I'm so happy you came!" Jules squealed jumping out of Scott's passenger side and hugging Madison. "Our dad's going to love you!"

As much as Jake had said the same thing to her on their drive over, hearing Jules also say it made Madison feel less nervous. "Let's hope so!" She smiled.

The house their father lived in was a beautiful home in an older subdivision on the outskirts of Meaford. His road winded along the shores of Georgian Bay while his house sat directly across the street from it.

"Is this where you guys grew up?" Madison asked as they approached the front door.

Jake nodded as he took her hand in his.

Signaling that they had arrived, Jake gave a courtesy knock as he opened the front door. Inside was stunning; open concept and tastefully decorated. It was one massive room with the odd beam here or there for structural support. Directly to her right was a sitting area with floor to ceiling bookshelves, to her left was the bathroom and stairs to the second floor. Past that was the living room and across from there was the kitchen with a large buffet. From the front door you could see straight to the back door where their dad stood in front of the barbeque. Upon seeing them, he instantly smiled and walked inside.

"Hey kiddos," He beamed and hugged both Jake and Jules tightly. He gave Scott a hug before turning to Madison. "I know we're just meeting, but I'm a hugger and I feel like I've heard so much about you that I know you already."

Madison opened her arms, "I'm a hugger, too."

"It's a pleasure to finally meet you, Madison. I'm William." he said pulling back and shaking her hand.

"The pleasure is all mine." She smiled. Looking at William, it was easy to see where Jake had gotten his good looks from; they were the spitting image of one another, William just had salt and pepper hair.

As they walked further into the house, there was a small front foyer table that lined the side of the stairs, and Madison spotted a photograph of a woman she knew had to be their mother. Similarly, to Jake and their father, Jules looked identical to their mother. Next to that picture was a family photograph of the four of them and based on how old Jake and Jules looked in it, Madison assumed it was probably one of the last ones they have of all of them together.

"Can I get you something to drink, Madison?" William asked walking into the kitchen.

"What are you drinking?" Madison asked.

"A Guinness for right now,"

"I'd love one of those if you have another," she answered. "Thank you for having me over for dinner," Madison said putting the bottles of wine on the kitchen buffet. "Jake wouldn't tell me whether you liked white or red, so I brought both."

"That was very kind of you, but you didn't need to do that!" He handed Madison her Guinness before examining the bottles. Smiling, he said, "Excellent choices, though. Thank you, this red will be great with our steaks."

Once everyone had a drink, they migrated to the patio in the backyard. On the table William had set out a spinach and artichoke dip with a plate of vegetables and crackers surrounding it.

Scott was still clearly hungover, and everyone laughed as they watched him struggle with the first few sips of his beer.

"I'll never turn down a drink with you, William," Scott said. "Even when I'm hurting."

The conversation throughout the night stayed light and Madison never felt like she was in the 'hot seat' with William. If anything, Madison felt extremely comfortable with Jake's dad and thoroughly enjoyed talking with him. They bonded over William's hiking stories and Madison marveled over them. When William found out where Madison and Jake had hiked earlier in the day, he told the story of how he had proposed to their mother and about one of their first dates to that lookout. Madison admired how William brought their mother, whose name she later learned was Patricia, up. It was never in sadness and it never changed the mood of their conversations - if anything it embraced her and her memory. Madison also couldn't help but notice that William still wore his wedding ring; like it was a permanent fixture on his hand.

It pained her, as she sat there amongst Jake, Jules and William, to think of the loss they had all gone through, and were still going through, when Patricia passed away. She couldn't imagine how lost they must have felt, but, somehow, they'd been able to find themselves and become a strong familial unit once again.

William was warm and inviting and Madison could tell that he was an excellent father. He had a unique bond with his children and Madison could see why they made weekly trips to visit him. Not to mention that he was an excellent chef. William had made delicious steaks, vegetable skewers and roasted sweet potatoes for them, and it was one of the best steaks Madison had ever had.

It was obvious to Madison after spending the evening with William and hearing him talk about his late wife, why he couldn't be with anyone else. She could tell that he was the kind of man that could only ever truly love one woman, and Madison had the feeling that Jake was a lot like his father.

Chapter Ten

Things were going extremely well for Madison and she couldn't help but feel that, given the circumstances, moving to Meaford had been the best decision she could have made. Not only meeting Jake but starting fresh in Meaford had helped Madison cope and sort through Annie's death on her own. Madison's parents still didn't fully understand why she needed to get away from home, despite how many times she told them, but for her it felt like people who knew what had happened made Madison feel even more guilty – even if they didn't mean to make her feel that way. People would say something like, 'We heard about what happened and we're so sorry.' Then, give Madison a look that screamed, 'but *you* were the one driving, weren't you?' Or at least Madison saw it that way, and she knew that she needed time away from having those experiences anytime she left the house. Had Madison stayed in Mississauga, she probably wouldn't have made the gains of overcoming the loss of Annie and its grief like she had in Meaford.

The weather that week had been spectacular meaning the grass at Middleton was thick and in constant need of cutting. When she wasn't working, she flipped between spending her evenings with Jake, in solitude, or with Jake, Jules, and Scott. While she clearly enjoyed spending time with Jake, she didn't want to start spending every second of every day with him now just because they were dating, and neither did he. As much of an extrovert as she was, Madison relished her alone time and was happy that Jake felt the same way.

It felt like the more time they spent together, and the time they spent apart, the more they learned how much they genuinely were alike. Of course, Madison and Jake had their differences, but they were good differences; the kind of differences that created growth or motivation in a partner.

Madison was looking forward to seeing what was in store for their relationship, but based on everything that had happened so far, she knew only good things were to come – starting with Drew and Evelyn's wedding.

While Madison wasn't exactly looking forward to attending initially, now she found that it was all she could think about. She had grown such a fond admiration and respect for Drew and Evelyn since she first met them that she couldn't imagine *not* being at their wedding, and being able to go with Jake was just a bonus.

Knock. Knock. Knock.

Madison looked herself over in the mirror one more time before leaning closer to it so she could check her teeth. Turning half-way around to make sure her dress wasn't accidentally tucked in someplace it shouldn't be, she smiled at herself because she felt beautiful. The dress she had bought for the wedding was black with red, pink, and white floral patterns spread across it. She accented the dress with a thick white belt around her waist, pulling the dress slightly tighter on her, making it more form fitting. It had short sleeves off her shoulder and hung right above her knees. It was modest, yet elegant and Madison couldn't help but feel sexy wearing it. Not to mention the manicure and pedicure she gave herself earlier that morning only adding to her confidence. When she saw that her dress wasn't in her underwear, she walked towards the front door.

Jake stood on the porch with a bouquet of flowers in his hands and honestly looked like a model. He wore fitted beige pants with a grey suit jacket, a light blue dress shirt and a midnight blue tie.

"Wow. You look stunning." he said as he kissed her cheek.

She blushed. "You do, too."

"I can't take any credit for it. Jules picked it out a few months ago," he said handing her the bouquet.

"Well, she did an excellent job. Thank you for the flowers. Just let me put them in water quickly."

Madison walked back into the kitchen and pulled scissors out of a drawer so she could cut around the bouquet's cellophane. She brought the flowers to the sink and cut the bottom stems off before opening the packet of flower food and emptying it into a vase. "How was your morning?" she asked filling the vase with water.

Jake leaned against the kitchen counter across from her. "Pretty uneventful. I was missing my right-hand lady."

She playfully rolled her eyes at him. "Doubtful. Were you able to nap at all? It's going to be a long night if you weren't able to…."

"A little, but I've had a few coffees that should help keep me awake. How was your morning?"

Madison set the vase of flowers on the kitchen table. "Good. I just did some self-care and gave myself a manicure and pedicure. What are you looking at?" Madison asked when she caught Jake staring at her.

Jake laughed. "You." He pushed himself off the counter and walked towards her. Cupping her face, he kissed her lustfully. Madison pulled him closer and feeling the heat from his body made her lightheaded.

"You have no idea how badly I don't want this to stop," she said between kisses.

"Then let's just stay here," he replied squeezing his arms tighter around her.

"And miss the wedding?"

"Sure."

"Jake-"

"How about being fashionably late?"

Madison pulled back and gave him a disapproving look. "*You* showing up fashionably late could work, but *me* showing up fashionably late? That's a hard no."

"Fashionably early it is!" he said pecking her cheek as he took her hand and led her to the front door. "Do you have everything you need?"

"I do now," she said in a cheesy voice.

"Me too," he replied while squeezing her hand a couple of times in agreeance.

Drew and Evelyn's wedding venue was the family farm Evelyn grew up on and where her parents still lived. As soon as Jake turned his truck onto their sideroad, signs for parking were in almost every neighbours' yard. Madison was impressed and surprised with how gracious their neighbours were with allowing people to park their cars in their fields, but she also thought it was a bit overkill. There couldn't be *that* many people showing up, could there?

"There sure is a lot of parking!" Madison exclaimed. "How many houses have we passed already that have signs? Ten?"

"At least ten. Hey, we kept trying to tell you how big of a deal their wedding was going to be, you know."

"I know, but this is still surprising. This is not how weddings happen in the city."

"What? You city folk are crazy! Weddings like these are the best!" He teased. "How's your footwear? Their driveway's long, but if your shoes aren't great, I can drop you off closer and then park the truck?"

"That's very sweet, but they're fine. I only wear shoes that I can walk in."

"Hmm," Jake smiled.

"What?"

He pulled his truck into a nearby field. "I'm not going to say what I'm thinking because I don't want to scare you off."

Madison's heart stopped with excitement, but she knew there wasn't anything he could say that would scare her off.

After parking the truck, Jake walked around to her door and opened it. He stuck out his arm in a gentlemanly gesture for Madison to link hers through. He had done it so casually it was as if they'd done it a hundred times before. Madison's heart felt like it was growing a thousand times bigger the more time they spent together, so she knew that tonight was going to be a good night.

Even though they parked in a neighbour's field, it was still a 200-meter walk before they got to Ben and Kate's driveway. But as they began up the laneway, Madison could already see how picturesque and fairy tale like the wedding was going to be. The driveway was long and winding, with aged trees the entire way up to the house and barn which were positioned at the top of a small hill. Not only was everything so naturally beautiful from how green and perfectly manicured things were, but there were tall standing vases of sunflowers and wildflowers between each of the trees, and Christmas lights were strung along the bases of each tree as well. Even though it was daylight, Madison could already see how beautiful it was going to look later that evening.

"I went to the bank yesterday and took out some cash for the bar," she said squeezing his arm. "Not that I'm trying to get you drunk-"

"Which I'd be perfectly fine with," He cut in winking at her. "But not to worry, it's an open bar. They do have a donation box, though."

"A donation box? I've never heard of that before."

"Yeah, they didn't have a registry, and they adamantly asked for no gifts, but if people felt like they *needed* to contribute something they can put money into the donation box at the bar for Merry and the caterers."

"That's an interesting idea. How would they know who donated and who didn't, and then who to thank?"

"I don't know. I mean, it's not what I would do, but it's what they want."

"Oh, and what would you do?" Madison asked intrigued.

Jake half laughed and half coughed. "You were fast on that. Wow. Uh, well, I'm just spit balling here because I haven't spent a lot of time thinking about it, but I think I'd just fill up a canoe with ice and beer and let people have at it."

"A canoe?"

"Or a toilet. A large toilet. That's way more redneck than a canoe, right?"

"Well, if it's the latter, count me out!" she giggled but stopped in her tracks when they had crested the hill of the driveway. "Oh, wow! It's breathtaking."

Ben and Kate's farmhouse stood on the left side of the driveway and was a beautiful yellow and white side paneled home with a gorgeous wrap-around deck. The barn, which was adjacent to the house about 50-metres away, was painted exquisitely red with white trim. The space between the house and barn had six different food trucks facing each other, three on the house side and three on the barn side, forming a quasi-courtyard look. As they walked closer, they stopped to read a chalkboard sign:

Eat, drink and be merry.
No precise time.
Eat <u>whenever</u> you're hungry.

"Does that mean we could even eat during the ceremony?" Madison asked.

"I think so," he replied breathing in deeply. "I don't know about you, but the smells these trucks are creating are making me hungry again, and I just ate!"

"Me too!"

They walked past the trucks on the house side first and were pleasantly surprised to discover Mexican, Indian, and Wood-Fire Pizza options. Madison and Jake slowed as they passed each menu, quickly glancing them over and discussing what they would choose. It appeared that what they both thought looked the best was the same, so they decided to order their top two favourites so they could maximize their chances of trying as much of the menus as possible.

After they finished reading the wood-fire pizza's menu, they stopped abruptly. As they turned to walk across the semi courtyard towards the other food trucks, they saw how the rest of the property was set up for the wedding and were awe-struck. There was a sizable yard kitty-corner to the house and barn where dozens of white linen tables and chairs sat underneath large strings of vintage light bulbs that were strung through the big, old oak trees that lined the yard. The trees also had white linen draping down their sides that were blowing lightly in the wind. On each table, in either old milk bottles or mason jars, were smaller versions of the sunflower and wildflower bouquets that lined the driveway. In the back corner of the yard, a band had set up their equipment under a white tent, and in front of them was a sizeable dance floor where wood boards had been placed on top of the grass to make it even.

Madison beamed. "Alright, well, this is officially the most beautiful wedding I've ever been to."

"They've done a great job," Jake agreed.

"If that's where the reception will be, where's the ceremony supposed to take place?"

"I think in the barn. I don't see an altar out here and I know Drew built one."

"In the barn?" she asked appallingly.

Jake laughed. "It's not a working barn and hasn't been for over forty years. I mean, at some point the barn was genuinely used for farming purposes, but it hasn't been since Ben and Kate have lived here. The fields around us are rented to their neighbours who are organic dairy farmers, so the barn has sat empty for many years. Did you assume you'd be sitting with pigs or something?" He teased.

"I don't know what I thought, but if the whole town is expected to show up, how are they all going to fit in there?" she asked pointing to it.

"Not my wedding, not my problem." He smirked.

They continued walking towards where the remaining three food trucks were parked in front of the barn, and their mouths began to water even more: BBQ Meats, Sushi, and one truck's specialty was just desserts.

"Should we start with dessert?" Madison asked standing in front of its menu while eyeing the peanut butter chocolate cheesecake.

"Dessert first? Kids these days!" Merry exclaimed hurrying past them with two bags of ice in her arms. "Happy to see you came, hon. Come find me in the barn for some drinks!"

Jake looked at his watch. "It's getting close to ceremony time. How about we divide and conquer? I'll get dessert, you get us some drinks? Peanut butter chocolate cheesecake and crème brûlée, right?"

"Deal," she said nodding. "What kind of beer would you like?"

"Surprise me."

"Okay." She smiled and followed Merry up the grassy ramp.

Inside the barn, Madison was once again struck by the wedding's gorgeous set-up. Directly in front of her was the aisle with an assortment of flower petals spread down it. White chairs sat on either side of the aisle in rows of ten. Madison quickly did the math, and one hundred and ten people would be able to sit comfortably inside the barn during the ceremony. Plus give or take another fifty standing around the chairs and at the back of the barn. Around each of the beams in the barn, more Christmas lights were strung from the floor to the ceiling and connected overhead as well. At the end of the barn was a beautiful altar wrapped in white linen, and more sunflower and wildflower bouquets surrounded it.

To the left of Madison, Merry worked tirelessly behind the bar and its set-up was also very impressive. The bar itself looked made and Madison could only assume Drew or Ben constructed it. It was in the shape of a 'U' with an elongated horizontal section, plus a raised shelf on top of it so drinks could be placed there while Merry and the other barmaids had things underneath. Behind that were four half skids with four kegs' taps running through the open slits. Above the taps, the slits were filled in with various other pieces of wood, so it was a flush surface where *'E + D's Beer Bar'* was written in rustic white paint. To the right of Merry was an extra table filled with an outrageous amount of wine and hard liquor bottles.

"There's enough wine and beer here for two towns!" Madison exclaimed as Merry opened a bag of ice and poured it into a keg that wasn't attached to the beer bar.

"The beer bar's pretty neat though, huh?"

"Very cool, but they're four kegs hooked up to it, but I see you're pouring ice into another garbage bin with another keg?"

"Oh yeah. This is the lighter stuff for when youse finish the heavier beers off," she said thumbing towards the taps.

Madison was shocked. How much beer were people going to drink? "What kind of beer is there?"

"An IPA Drew and Evelyn made – they took a course or somethin'. Canned Sunset is an organic beer from Outlaw Brewery in Southampton, Mountain Lager is from Sidelaunch in Collingwood, and the Kolsh is from Killanan Brewing Company in Owen Sound. The light stuff's just Canadian."

"Wow, that's a great selection. Can I start with two of the IPAs Drew and Evelyn made, please?"

After getting hers and Jake's beers, Madison made her way back to the dessert truck. Surrounding a standing table on a patch of grass in the reception area, she saw Jake, Jules, Scott, and William.

Jules looked stunning in a beautifully fitted navy dress and gold shawl, with her hair tied back in a perfect bun. Scott wore light grey pants and jacket, a white-collared shirt and a deep burgundy tie covered in flowers, while William wore a dark grey suit, light blue shirt and a dark blue bowtie.

"You look gorgeous!" Jules sang when Madison approached.

"Thank you, you all look incredible. I love your dress, Jules."

"This old thing?" She smirked.

"Which dessert would you like to start with?" Jake asked referring to the two that were next to him on the table.

"Definitely the cheesecake."

Jake handed her the peanut butter and chocolate cheesecake and took the pint of beer from her.

"What did you get?"

"An IPA that Drew and Evelyn made," Madison replied.

"Their own IPA? I remember them doing a course a few months ago. Is the beer good?" Scott asked.

Both Jake and Madison took a swig and nodded.

Scott rested his hand on Jules' back. "Do you want one? How about you, William?"

"Yes, thanks, Scott." Jules and William said.

As they finished their desserts and drinks, they made small talk about how wonderful the weather had turned out to be and about all the charming details Drew and Evelyn had put into their big day.

"This is the coolest, most thoughtful and most beautiful wedding I've ever been to. There's attention to detail for every little thing," Madison praised.

"I knew it would be beautiful, but I didn't expect it to be *this* beautiful," Jules concurred.

"We should probably go and find a spot inside for the ceremony." William offered looking at his watch.

The barn was practically full by the time they walked inside, but luckily, they were able to find a row of five seats together.

"Is it bad that I want to have those desserts again before we move onto the next food truck?" Madison whispered to Jake as they sat down.

"I was thinking the same thing. I think I'm going to have to have at least three more of each before the night's out," he replied. Taking a sip of his beer, he leaned back in his chair and nonchalantly rested his arm behind her.

Madison's heart fluttered and she nuzzled closer into him. Within five minutes, the quiet murmuring throughout the barn stopped, and an acoustic guitar began to play.

"Hey, I know this song," Madison said quietly in his ear. "But it isn't normally acoustic, so I can't place it. Damn, what's its name?" She leaned forward in her seat to see if Jules had an idea, but upon seeing her expression Madison could tell that Jules was just as stumped as she was.

"Oh my god! It's 'Another One Bites the Dust' by Queen!" Jules whispered a few seconds later.

Towards the back of the barn, they heard Robbie's voice begin singing along with the guitar. *"And another one gone, and another one gone, another one bites the dust!"*

The barn erupted in laughter and clapping just as Drew appeared at the barn's entrance with his mother. Once he was spotted, the laughter and clapping turned to hollering, and Drew smiled from ear to ear. As Drew and his mother walked towards the altar, more wedding guests joined Robbie in singing the lyrics to Queen's hit. Drew and his mother half sang, and half laughed as they walked arm in arm.

Once he reached the altar, kissed his mother on the cheek, and was in place, the guitarist began playing another song to signal the groomsmen and bridal party's entrance.

Drew and Evelyn hadn't made their bridal party buy specific suits or dresses and they had the freedom to wear whatever they wanted. Despite it not being traditional, Madison loved the idea and thought everyone actually looked better than if they were all wearing the same thing. Once everyone was standing in place, the guitarist began to play a soft, beautiful acoustic melody, signaling to everyone that they needed to stand because Evelyn was ready to walk down the aisle towards her future husband.

Evelyn looked picturesque as she appeared in the barn's entrance with Ben and Kate on either side of her. Evelyn's dress was stunning with a boat neck cut, and lace down the bodice and trailing to the floor. Her hair was tied back and pinned in a messy bun with baby's breath flowers intertwined. Once they reached the end of the aisle, Evelyn kissed her parents, and each of them hugged Drew before sitting down next to his parents.

Neither Drew nor Evelyn could contain their smiles as they stared lovingly into one another's eyes.

"You look gorgeous," Drew said smiling and wiping a tear from his eye.

"Can I kiss him yet?" Evelyn asked and everyone laughed.

The ceremony was no longer than ten minutes, with the officiant giving a very abbreviated and hilarious version of Drew and Evelyn's love story. Hearing it made Madison's heart leap with happiness, not only for the newlyweds, but for what was blossoming between her and Jake. She couldn't help but feel that, for the first time since Annie's death, her life might be back on track.

After Drew and Evelyn kissed and walked back up the aisle as husband and wife, Robbie shouted, "And now it's beer o'clock!"

The barn erupted even louder than before, and it was obvious that people were ready to party.

Jake leaned into Madison. "Do you want to go for a walk?"

"I would love that," Madison responded. She had been craving some alone time with him and knew a walk would give them just that.

"Should we grab a couple more drinks?"

"Yes, Their IPA was delicious!"

He took her hand. "Come on, we might just be able to beat the line."

"How did youse like the IPA?" Merry asked stretching out her arms to take their glasses as they approached. "Refill or somethin' else?"

"Refill," they said in unison, smiling.

"Drew and Evelyn could go into the brewing business!" Jake responded, quickly slipping a $50 bill into Merry's tip jar.

Even with her back turned, Merry could tell what Jake was doing and shouted, "You take that out of there right now and either put it back into your wallet or in the donation box, mister! I don't pay you to cut my grass and shovel my driveway just for you to give me my own money back!"

"It's Madison's money," Jake lied.

Merry turned around with their beers and set them on the tabletop. "You can't start paying someone when they're ten only to stop when they're twenty-five!"

"But you can, Merry! I have a job, I own a house and a truck, and I have the prettiest date here. Things are going well for me." He winked.

"You two sure make one hot couple! Your babies are going to be damned good looking!" Merry smiled at Jake knowing what she had said made him uncomfortable. "But you can't lie for crap. Now take your money back, Jake, and do as your told."

"Yes, mam," Jake said smiling. Putting his hand on Madison's lower back, he steered her towards the exit of the barn.

"So, talking about babies makes you squirm?" Madison asked as they walked through the reception area towards where the band had set up.

"Actual babies? No, they're great. But talking about how good looking my future babies will be with the girl I just started dating? That makes me squirm."

Madison's heart started pounding so loudly she was sure Jake could hear it. For whatever reason, the label of them dating hadn't occurred to her yet. But they were dating, weren't they? Her mind began to swirl with all the questions that come when beginning to officially date someone, but Madison decided to not overthink things and just stick to the babies topic. "Do you want kids someday, though?"

"Of course. Who doesn't? It's just terrifying, you know?"

She stopped walking and stared at him awe-struck. "Do you realize that you are unlike any man I've ever met before?"

He stood jubilantly. "Tell me more!"

She knew he was teasing, but she was serious. "Well, you talk for one thing. You're honest and don't shy away from talking about hard subjects. You cut and shovel the driveway of an old lady - no offense to Merry, you're close to your sister, and your best friend is someone whom you've known your entire life. You wear your heart on your sleeve, you just said we were dating, and you just made every other man out there that doesn't want kids look like a chump." She took a step closer to him. "I could go on all night."

He took her hand and began walking again. "I wouldn't discourage that, you know."

Madison rolled her eyes and smiled. "Where are you taking me by the way?" she asked as they were about to enter a forested area along what looked like an ATV path.

"There's a nice pond at the end of this trail." Madison looked at him with a curious expression on her face as to how he would know that. "Evelyn used to babysit Jules and me when we were younger."

"She used to babysit you, but she doesn't seem that much older than us?" Madison asked taking a sip of her beer.

"She's not; she's only three years older than me."

"You must have had a mad crush on her then?"

Jake laughed. "Maybe I would have if our parents weren't such good friends and Drew wasn't so terrifying."

Madison was shocked. "Drew? Terrifying?"

"Hey, when you're thirteen years old, your babysitter's boyfriend *is* terrifying – even if it is Drew."

Madison stopped walking. "Wait, when you were thirteen you needed a babysitter? How bad of a kid were you?"

He squeezed her hand and they continued walking. "'Babysitter' probably isn't the best word to describe what Evelyn was, but at the same time 'babysitter' is the best word. I was thirteen when our mom died, and our dad didn't want us spending too much time alone once he had to go back to work, so Evelyn would either come over or we'd come here and explore the property with her, her sisters, and Drew. Scott would usually come too since he was always at our house."

"Oh, Jake. I'm so sorry. I didn't realize."

Jake squeezed her hand again. "I know, and it's okay. I think by now you know that Jules, my dad, and I can talk about our mom and be okay."

She leaned her head against his arm as they walked. "I do and I admire that. But I still feel sad because of what you lost. No one should lose their mother, especially so young."

Jake stopped walking and stood facing her. He lifted her chin with his finger. "And no one should lose their best friend, especially so young."

He kissed her lightly but pulled away when he heard voices. "Do you hear that?" he asked.

Madison nodded and they looked around them. Aside from the path they were on and the clearing up ahead, it was dense forest. Jake walked towards the clearing, purposefully trying to keep hidden behind the trees as he peeked his head out.

"So much for my plan," he whispered and pointed to where Drew and Evelyn were getting their wedding photos taken.

Ahead of them was a decently sized pond with a beautiful dock that went out thirty feet from the shore. Massive trees circled around it and a gazebo was on the far end near where there was sand and Muskoka chairs. Drew and Evelyn stood on the dock kissing as their photographer snapped pictures.

"You weren't kidding about it being beautiful back here!" she whispered back.

"Are you hungry? We could head back and try something different or just get dessert again?" Jake asked draining the last of his beer.

"Yes! Hm as tempting as dessert again is, maybe something from the wood-fire pizza truck?"

Once they made their way out of the forest, they quickly saw how the amount of wedding guests had grown exponentially in size while they were on their walk. It was as if every table and chair had people occupying them, while hundreds more were standing or sitting on the grass around them. Anticipating this, Drew and Evelyn had baskets of blankets people could spread on the grass and sit on with their food and drink as if having a picnic.

Despite the enormous amount of people in line for each of the food trucks, the lines moved surprisingly quickly and within no time Madison and Jake were standing with their pizza in search of somewhere to sit.

"I don't mind sitting on the grass, even if all of the blankets are being used." Madison offered.

"It might come to that, but knowing my dad, Jules and Scott, they'll have snagged a table and saved us seats," he said reassuringly. "Keep your eyes peeled, though, we just need to find them."

It didn't take long and within a few moments they spotted Jules waving them over to the table they were sitting at.

"You would not!" Jules laughed as they approached.

"I would so!" Scott countered.

"I'd pay to see it!" William added.

Jake pulled out Madison's chair. "Pay to see what?"

"Scott dance to Beyonce's 'Single Ladies' tonight like they do in the music video," Jules answered.

"Well, he's already got the leotards at home so the dance should come pretty easily," Jake jokingly added.

The five of them sat talking and laughing in the warm, afternoon sun, drinking beers, and rotating between which food trucks they ordered from. The afternoon seemed to be slipping by quickly and Madison couldn't help a sinking feeling in her stomach knowing that the day was almost half over. She was feeling so happy and content that she truly wanted it to last forever.

Many people came to the table they were sitting at to say hello to William, his children, and Scott, and Jake always made sure he introduced Madison before the conversation got too carried away, and Madison genuinely appreciated it. The more time she spent with him the more she realized how much of a true gentleman he was.

As the night continued, the conversation between them remained light and fun, and Madison felt even more comfortable with Jake's dad than the previous weekend. William was highly likeable, and as the night wore on, and the more time she spent with him, the more similarities she saw between him and his children: the smile creases on their cheeks, their noses, and their eyes. Even some of their mannerisms were the same; the way they laughed and used their hands when telling a story.

Drew and Evelyn had reappeared from taking their photos at some point in the evening but were kept busy making the rounds and saying hello to all their guests. Madison watched them in awe as they moved from one group to another, calm and relaxed. She'd never witnessed a bride and groom pay such undivided attention to so many different people while appearing so laid-back, happy, and having the time of their lives. While Drew and Evelyn *should* be having the time of their lives since it was *their* special day, Madison had only attended weddings where the bride and groom were stressed, anxious, and overwhelmed – and with half the guests. She didn't know how they were managing but admired them for it.

As the afternoon turned into evening, the reception and surrounding area became even more full, which shocked Madison. Now she understood why there were six food trucks, so many kegs of beer, and multiple bottles of wine and other liquor. With the sun dipping into the horizon, the Christmas lights that had been set up around the property were now turned on and, somehow, Drew and Evelyn's wedding became even more fairytale-like.

"Excuse me," Ben said into the microphone with his wife, Kate, beside him. "Can I get everyone's attention, please?" The voices of all the enthusiastic wedding guests quieted down, and the parents of the bride began their speech. Theirs and Drew's parents' speeches were sentimental and heart-warming. It was apparent that both sets of parents were beyond happy their families were officially becoming one, and so happy with their child's choice of partner. Connor and Evelyn's sisters, Victoria and Charlotte, did a joint speech which had everyone in fits of laughter and tears of joy.

Garbage bins of sparklers were set-up around the grounds and guests were told to grab one for Drew and Evelyn's first dance. To light them, the caterers were ready and equipped with lighters. After a few moments, the band began to play an acoustic version of Matchbox Twenty's 'Overjoyed' and with the ambiance of day, the venue, the song and the sparklers, it was an absolutely magical moment. Guests were told to take more sparklers once Drew's mother and Ben joined them on the dance floor for their joint parent dance to another acoustic version of a song: James Taylor's 'How Sweet It Is To Be Loved By You.'

Once the official dances were over, the newlyweds made their way to the microphone.

"We appreciate the lovely words from our parents, Connor, Victoria, and Charlotte more than we will ever be able to express, but that's it for speeches." She grabbed Drew's hand. "What we have to say to each other is just for our ears and will be done without such a wonderful and beautiful audience such as yourself."

Drew kissed her forehead. "Thank you all so much for coming and celebrating our day with us! The evening is yours!"

Anyone that was sitting was now standing, and all the attendees clapped and cheered. The band was geared up and ready to go and immediately began to play Sam Cooke's 'Having a Party'. No one returned to their seats, but rather moved towards the dance floor or just started dancing where they were standing.

Jake took Madison's hand and led her towards the dance floor. There were a lot of people and the spacing was tight, so

Jake pulled her close and led her to the rhythm. When the right opportunity arose, and there was space between the other dancers, he sent her out, brought her back in, and twirled her all while in perfect sync to the beat. Madison had been turned on all night by Jake and how things were unfolding between them, but after witnessing his confidence and ability on the dance floor, she was ready to burst.

Once the song had finished, and the band started to play 'At Last' by Etta James, Jake kissed her cheek and said, "I'll go get us some more drinks."

"Not so fast, Mr. Dancing Shoes!" Madison called after him and grabbed his hand before he got too far away.

"Oh no, no, no, you don't want to slow dance with me. Trust me; I've got two left feet when it comes to slow music."

She pulled him closer, wrapped her right arm around his neck and brought their held hands between their shoulders. "After how you just spun me around? I don't believe you have two left feet for a second! But even if it is true, my feet will survive."

Madison hummed along as she rested her head on his shoulder and they swayed to the classic love song. Their night was turning out perfectly and Madison felt so happy, giddy almost, as she held onto Jake tightly, and he to her.

However, as time passed, despite there being lots of other people on the dance floor, Madison began to feel like they were being watched. Of course, to an extent, they were, and Madison wasn't ignorant to the fact that people would be watching Jake and his new lady friend at Drew and Evelyn's wedding; it was a small town after all. But the feeling now was stronger than ever, and Madison was beginning to feel self-conscious. She didn't want to lift her head off Jake's shoulder and ruin the moment they were having by looking around, so she just closed her eyes.

As the song slowed towards its finish, Madison slowly opened her eyes and was horrified. There was a clear line of sight from where Jake and Madison stood on the dance floor to the other side of the property, and there, in the shadows of the barn, stood Annie.

Madison's body went stiff, and her head snapped upright. "Annie?" she half-yelled.

Everyone dancing around them stopped and looked at her and Jake.

"Annie?" Jake repeated leaning his head down to meet Madison's eyes.

Her eyes drifted to Jake for a split second before she was drawn again to where she thought she had just seen Annie standing. Annie was now walking away from the barn and down the small hill behind it, towards the bathrooms.

"I have to go to the bathroom!" Madison said urgently, pulling away from Jake.

"Is everything alright?" he asked, but Madison had already disappeared among the crowded dance floor.

She half walked, half jogged her way through the reception area, bypassing the food trucks, and was standing by the side of the barn where she had last seen Annie in no time. She followed the small hill along the barn and down towards the fancy outhouses but didn't see anyone. Thirty feet in front of where the bathrooms' fronts faced, were half a dozen white rocking chairs for people to sit if there was a line for the bathroom, but all of them were empty. Madison quickly walked along the bathroom stalls looking at the vacancies but saw that none of them were occupied. Behind the bathrooms was a cornfield and Madison frantically looked between the stalks to try and see if anyone was there, but she was alone. In the distance, she could faintly hear the band playing 'Jailhouse Rock' by Elvis Presley.

"Annie?" Madison called, as she weaved her way between the outhouses and rocking chairs.

She froze when she heard rustling in the cornfield. Twenty feet in front of her she saw a woman emerge that definitely wasn't Annie.

Madison sighed. "Sorry, you scared me. I'm looking for someone, did you happen to see anyone else in the cornfield?"

Nothing about the woman's face indicated that she had heard Madison, so she tried again. "I'm sorry, but this is important, was there anyone else in the cornfield?"

"He's never going to love you," the woman seethed walking towards Madison.

Her eyebrows furrowed. "Excuse me?"

"Jake's still mine. You know that, right?" The woman was now standing only a few feet from Madison.

"Becca," Madison whispered backing up. She looked around hoping that someone would be nearby and could help if things escalated, but no one waa. "Look, I don't want to start anything; I was just back here looking for someone."

"Oh, I'm pretty sure you do. I mean, why else would you come running after me?"

"What?" Madison asked confused. I came running after Annie.

Becca now stood a few inches from Madison's face and grabbed her arm. "Do you know how many other women he's had before you, just trying to get over me? What makes you think you're so special?"

In that moment, when Becca grabbed hold of her arm, something snapped inside of Madison and she no longer felt the need for someone else's help. Madison stared directly into Becca's eyes and calmly replied, "Let go of me."

"He treats ya'll like gold until he goes to bed with you and then realizes that you're not me."

Remaining calm, Madison repeated, "I'm only going to ask you one more time; let go of my arm."

While Becca let go of her arm, her face remained inches from Madison's. Laughing she said, "You're just another notch on his belt." Growing more serious, she continued, "So you might as well just go back to where you came from because you don't belong here."

"No, you don't belong here," Madison spat back and stepped away from Becca. "Which is why *I* was invited to this wedding and I'm Jake's date, *not* you. You should leave before you ruin Drew and Evelyn's big day."

Madison turned quickly and headed back towards the barn; her body clenched, bracing for impact in case Becca decided to chase after her. However, when Madison glanced over her shoulder, Becca was nowhere to be seen.

Reaching the side of the barn, Madison checked one last time for Becca and when she didn't see her, her knees buckled. She grabbed hold of the barn for support, otherwise she would have fallen to the ground. Keeling over, she rested her hands on her knees and took several deep breaths.

"There you are!" She heard Jake say approaching her. "Jules requested 'Single Ladies' so we can all witness Scott danc– Hey, are you okay?"

Madison was still bent over, head facing the grass, when she saw him place their drinks beside her feet.

"What's the matter? Are you feeling sick? If I'd known, I would have come to the bathroom with you rather than get us drinks," he said crouching down, so they were face to face. He gently placed a hand on her back but recoiled when Madison shot up and cringed at the feel of his hand.

"Don't!" she shouted.

"Whoa, okay." His arms shot in the air defensively and she could see the pain and bewilderment spread across his face. "I'm sorry. What can I do to help?"

Madison knew she shouldn't have snapped at him, but she was having a hard time comprehending what had just happened with Becca. Madison wasn't a big drinker, but she was fairly certain that she hadn't imagined Becca being there or their conversation, but where had she vanished to? Madison knew she needed more time to make sense of what had just happened, and not to let the alcohol get the best of her, and knew she needed to leave.

"I need to go home," she said as she walked past Jake and up the side of the barn.

He looked at his watch. "Okay, but I'm in no state to drive and the shuttle doesn't start for another thirty minutes."

"That's fine; I'll call a cab," she said continuing up the hill.

"Wait, can you hold on a second, please?" He stood in front of her now, blocking her path.

"What?" She snapped again.

The pain on his face was even more evident now. "All the cab drivers in town are here tonight - as guests. No one would pick up even if you called. Look, if you really want to leave, I can call my friend that's a police officer and is on duty tonight and he can come and pick us up."

"No, you stay. Tonight's a big night for your friends. I'll be fine."

Jake walked towards Madison and tentatively took her hand. "It is, but they won't even know I'm gone. It's you that I'm worried about. If you'll let me, I'd like to take you home to make sure that you're okay."

She shook her head dismissively. "Fine. Can we just go?"

Jake raised his eyebrows, clearly surprised by her attitude but didn't acknowledge it. Instead, he just took a step back, allowing her to lead the way. "After you," he said in a monotone voice.

Madison just nodded in response. She figured it was best now for her to keep her mouth shut rather than risk saying something else rude or hurtful.

As they walked down the driveway towards the road, Madison replayed what happened with Becca in her head. Had it really been Becca that Madison had followed and not Annie? Obviously, it couldn't have been Annie because Annie is dead, but she knew what her best friend looked like and she was sure it was her. However, if it was Becca, how come other guests didn't see her? It was a massive wedding full of people that knew her. Not to mention that it was common knowledge around town that Becca was no longer friends with Drew and Evelyn ever since her and Jake broke up, so how could she have been there and gone unnoticed by other guests? Also, why weren't there other people by the bathrooms? There were too many people at the wedding to have had no one witness their exchange. And how could Madison have chased after Becca wanting to start something when Madison had no idea what Becca even looked like! Over and over the conversation played in Madison's head and she still couldn't make sense of it. She knew Becca was just trying to get under her skin and what bothered Madison the most was that it was working. Why did Madison have to chase after something that could never have been real? It couldn't have been Annie, so why did Madison even think it was? None of this would be happening if she'd just stayed on the dance floor with Jake. Madison began to be more upset with herself for being so foolish thinking she had seen Annie than what had actually transpired between them. Becca had won against Jake and his emotions, and she had now won against Madison's, too.

They waited together in uncomfortable silence at the end of Ben and Kate's driveway. She could feel the air between them heavy with Jake's confusion. After a few moments, a police cruiser appeared down the road.

Jake took a deep breath. "Look, I'm not sure what's happened tonight for things to have gone as south as they have, and if you're not in the mood to talk about it tonight that's fine.

But I would still like to spend the night together, even if we're in separate rooms, I don't care, I just don't want to go to sleep so confused in separate houses."

Madison's features softened and she nodded. "You're right. If you still want to come back to my place, I would like that."

Jake stepped closer to Madison and gave a tentative smile. "I would like that."

"I'm sorry for how rude I was back there, but I've had too much to drink and am trying to process something that happened tonight. Can we talk about it tomorrow morning?"

Jake nodded just as the police cruiser stopped in front of them. He opened the backseat passenger door for Madison and hopped into the front seat. As Jake made small talk with Officer Craig in the front of the cruiser, Madison tuned them out as she stared out the window.

Chapter Eleven

Madison tossed and turned all night and had barely slept. She finally couldn't stand being so restless anymore and decided to get out of bed just before 7:00 AM. Trying to be as quiet as she could so Jake could still sleep; she brewed coffee and toasted a bagel. Just as she sat down on the couch with her breakfast and coffee, she heard rustling in the bedroom.

"Good morning," she said when Jake appeared in the doorframe. Embarrassed by how she had acted last night, she offered him an apologetic smile. Aside from her conversation with Becca, all Madison could remember from Drew and Evelyn's wedding was the hurt look on Jake's face when she had snapped at him.

"Good morning," he replied groggily wiping his eyes.

"There's fresh coffee in the pot." She offered.

Jake moaned as he walked over to the coffee pot and filled the mug Madison had left out on the counter for him.

Following behind him, she leaned against the counter. "I'm really sorry about last night, Jake. I'm sorry I snapped at you when you thought I was sick and put your hand on my shoulder, and I'm sorry that I gave you attitude as we were leaving. I'm also sorry that I didn't explain what was going on, but, honestly, I was a little too drunk and didn't want my emotions going even more berserk. Thank you for giving me the night to digest it and not prying."

Jake took a deep breath and was about to reply but abruptly stopped when he heard an unusual sound. In the distance, it sounded as if a car was speeding down her gravel road towards them. Within seconds, Jake and Madison exchanged concerned looks because they realized that a car *was* barreling down her road and getting closer. Before they even knew what was happening, the vehicle had screeched to a halt in front of her cottage. They frowned at each other when they heard a door slam and footsteps pound up her porch. Madison jumped at the sound of the front door being hit.

"I know you're in there, Jake! Come on out and let's finally settle this - man to man," Mike Smith shouted, and then his footsteps pounded back down the porch steps.

"What is he doing here?" Jake asked. "How does he even know where you live?"

"I don't know," Madison replied, bewildered.

They walked into the front hallway and Jake hovered behind the front door while Madison went into the bathroom to peak out its small window. Mike paced in circles on her front lawn while clenching and unclenching his fists.

"What do you want, Mike?" Jake yelled through the door.

Now, another vehicle could be heard racing towards them and within seconds Scott's truck slid to a stop in front of her cottage.

"Get back in your car!" Scott yelled at Mike as he hopped out of his truck.

Jules got out of the passenger side. "The police are on their way, Mike."

Unfazed by their arrival, Mike was still pacing but was now rubbing his hands together like he was getting ready to punch something - or someone.

Scott stood ten feet away from Mike and Jules was right behind him. Her hand holding onto his forearm.

Madison tiptoed out of the bathroom and back into the front hallway. Her weight made one of the floorboards creak and Jake shot an aggravated look her way. When their eyes met, his features softened but his body remained tense. His face screamed an assortment of emotions ranging from embarrassment and vulnerability to shock and anger, and Madison felt even worse for how she had treated him last night.

"What's going on?" she whispered.

"I'm not sure, but just stay back from the door, okay?"

"The cops are on their way!" They heard Jules repeat.

"Does it look like I care?" They heard Mike shout.

"Do you remember if you locked the screen door last night?" Jake asked her, and Madison nodded.

He slowly unlocked the front door and carefully opened it.

Mike froze on the front lawn before he slowly turned to face them. His eyes shot daggers at Jake and Madison suddenly felt scared.

"What did you say to Becca last night?" Mike asked calmly.

"What?" Jake asked bewildered. "What are you talking about, Mike? I was at Drew and Evelyn's wedding last night which Becca was uninvited to."

Mike practically sprinted up the porch and once he was right in front of Jake, he aggressively tried to open the porch door. He rattled it a few times but thankfully the screen's lock didn't budge. Seconds later, Scott was behind Mike ready to pull him back down the porch if he tried anything more physical.

"Just calm down, Mike! I haven't seen or heard from Becca in months! To be honest, this is a bit much, coming to Madison's house and accusing me-"

"She's in the hospital."

Jake stopped talking. "What? How?"

"The wedding!" Mike shouted.

"Mike, she was uninvited! Drew and Evelyn spoke directly to her about it."

"Yeah, well, she said she'd been re-invited to the reception and left the house last night in a dress!"

"And you didn't think her being re-invited to two of my best friend's wedding was a bit odd?" Jake asked, his voice rising. "Why would she be re-invited?" he yelled.

Mike snapped and leapt at the screen door, smacking it hard with his hand. "Don't turn this around! This is your fault!"

Scott grabbed Mike and half threw, half pushed him down the porch steps. Clearly having good balance, Mike only stumbled a bit.

Not having flinched at the sudden attack, Jake replied in an even voice, "Nothing about what happened when Becca and I were dating, engaged or since we've broken up has been my fault, and whatever happened last night isn't my fault either."

Mike was now standing on the grass where he had been pacing earlier, while Scott stood on the bottom porch step. "She went to that wedding a person, and now she's a vegetable because of you!"

"*What* are you talking about?"

"Oh, have I got your attention now? Yeah, her car wrapped around a tree. If she dies, it'll be on you."

"I saw her," Madison half-shouted over them.

Jake slowly turned around.

"What do you mean you saw her?" he asked sounding hurt.

"This is what I was just about to explain-"

"What did you say to her?" He cut her off, his tone accusatory now.

Mike exploded at Madison, "You little-"

"HEY!" Jake snapped back around to face Mike on the grass. "You can say whatever you want to me and talk to me in whatever tone you want, but you cannot talk to her like that! Do you understand?"

"Becca's in critical condition, so I'll talk to her any god damned way I want," Mike spat.

At that moment, a police cruiser pulled into Madison's driveway.

"What seems to be the problem here?" the woman officer asked getting out of the driver's side.

"Why don't you ask her?" Mike replied pointing to Madison.

"I'm asking you," the officer said walking up to the porch.

"You know what happened to Becca last night, Officer Harlan, so I'm here just trying to figure out how it all happened."

"That's not your job, and this isn't the way we do it."

"Well, how nice of you to show up," Mike snarled.

"Why don't you ride with me back to the station?"

"I'm fine right where I am."

"That wasn't a question, Mike."

He let out a devilish laugh. "Of course, it wasn't. You're going to put me in the back of the cruiser while Jake gets to enjoy a lovely Sunday morning with his-"

Officer Harlan was a tall and muscular woman with broad shoulders, so when she walked up the porch steps and stood in front of Mike, essentially blocking his view of Jake and Madison, he abruptly stopped talking. "That's enough, Mike. Let's go."

"I ain't going anywhere with you," he said staring directly into her eyes. Shifting his weight so he could see past her at Jake and Madison, he continued "This isn't over."

He slowly took a few steps backwards before turning and walking back to his car. He aggressively slapped its hood before opening its door. Reversing quickly, gravel sprayed everywhere as he turned around and sped back up the road.

"Sorry about that Jake. I'll have an officer swing by here a few times over the next couple of days to check in and make sure things are okay, alright? But you call if there's any sign of trouble."

"Thank you, Officer Harlan."

"Y'all have a nice day now." She nodded at Madison before heading back to her cruiser.

"So that's what happened last night?" Jake whispered as Officer Harlan drove off. He still stood with his back to her and staring out the screen door. Only turning his head slightly to the right so he could see her through his peripheral vision.

Madison hesitated. "Yes. I...I was in shock. Like I was trying to say earlier, I needed time to digest the whole thing-"

Jake turned around now and cut her off. "*You* needed time to digest the whole thing? *What* whole thing? I'm sorry, because last time I checked you weren't engaged to Becca or had her or Mike trying to ruin your life for the past year."

Madison felt hurt by his words even though she knew he was right. Seeing how he was reacting now Madison knew she had made the wrong decision of not explaining what had happened last night to him. Had she known he would have reacted this way, she would have just told him everything, despite it not making sense to her. "Jake, you're right, but you must understand. The things she said were horrible and then she was just gone, like she'd never been there so, of course, I started to wonder if I'd made the whole thing up...."

Avoiding her eyes, he walked past her and into the bedroom.

Madison followed behind him. "Jake-"

"You should have just told me the truth last night."

"I know," Madison replied sheepishly standing in the door frame.

Ignoring that she was standing there watching him as he gathered his things, he rolled his clothes into a ball under his arm. Once he grabbed his shoes he stopped just as he past her, "Well, I guess it's a little late now, isn't it?"

Madison's breath caught. She knew Jake was mad, but she'd never heard his voice take such a snippy tone before. "Jake, I know I should have told you, but please just wait-"

Not listening to her, he continued towards the porch door.

Scott and Jules were now standing at the bottom of the front steps. Jake did not even acknowledge them as he walked past, and instead just walked towards Scott's truck, opened a backseat door, and got in.

Uncontrollable tears began to run down Madison's cheeks as she stood on the other side of the screen porch door.

Scott gave her a heartfelt look before heading towards his truck.

Jules whispered, "I'm so sorry, Madison. Are you going to be okay? Can I call you later?"

A million things were running through Madison's head. Unable to actually voice an answer, she just nodded at Jules.

As Madison watched Scott's truck pull away, she couldn't help but feel like this was the beginning of the end.

Madison began to struggle to breath the second Queens Lawn Cemetery came into view and her body froze as if she had been dropped into a pool of ice water. She immediately pulled onto the shoulder of the road and took several deep breaths. Physically, Madison's body was rejecting the idea of getting any closer to Annie's grave, but mentally Madison knew she had to.

After Jake got into Scott's truck and they drove away, Madison wasn't sure what to do with herself. She knew she needed to clear her head and that a long drive would provide her with that opportunity. She didn't know exactly where she was going to drive, while at the same time knew exactly where she needed to go. Madison hadn't been to Queens Lawn Cemetery since Annie's funeral a few months ago and it seemed like the only place for her to be.

Annie's funeral was in the beginning of spring, so the cemetery had been dreary and bland, but now that it was summer and there had been a decent amount of rain, Queens Lawn looked luscious. The flowerbeds were full and thriving, the grass was neatly manicured, and every headstone had a beautiful bouquet of flowers next to it. Madison's heart smiled knowing that Annie would have also thought it looked pretty.

The laneway into Queens Lawn was long and wound through big weeping willow trees. The cemetery itself wasn't overly big and, despite Madison having been a complete wreck the last time she had been there, she was still able to locate Annie's grave.

Tears ran down Madison's cheeks before she even realized she was crying, and her eyes became so blurry and wet that she had to pull over once again. Luckily where she stopped was close enough to where Annie lay that she decided that it would be best to just turn her car off there and walk the rest of the way.

Madison mechanically got out of her car and walked in the direction of the large Japanese maple tree she knew stood beside Annie's headstone.

Collapsing on the grass in front of it, minutes passed where she was sobbing so heavily that breathing became difficult again. Months of sadness, heartache, despair, guilt, and mourning came pouring out of Madison. Once she had calmed down, Madison sat quietly, listening to the birds chirping and picked at the grass by her feet. After a while, Madison worked up enough nerve to talk to Annie's grave and began to recount everything about the wedding, her encounter with Becca, and what happened earlier that morning with Mike.

"Jake was so hurt and then so angry when he realized I hadn't told him the truth last night. If I had, maybe Becca wouldn't be in the hospital right now. Maybe Jake would have been able to call someone who would have been able to find her before she got into her car. What happened to Becca is my fault and it's hard not to compare what happened to you and what happened to her. I mean, they're nothing alike while at the same time being everything alike because of me. Just when I think things are going well, I screw someone else's life up." Madison sighed heavily. "I'm so sorry, Annie. I would give anything to have traded spots with you that night, you know that, right? I just wish you were here. You know, I can't help but think that none of this would be happening if I just hadn't picked you up from the party that night."

"You know that's not true," a male voice said behind her.

Madison jumped at the sound of the familiar voice. "Patrick! What are you doing here?" She stood up quickly wiping her cheeks with her hands. Initially she felt embarrassed because he'd overheard her private conversation with Annie, but then she became angry that he had. "How long have you been standing there?" she asked accusingly.

Patrick was a few feet away from her and was holding a bouquet of daisies in his hands. "I didn't really hear anything except the last sentence. But I do come by every so often to drop these off," he said lifting the bouquet slightly before placing them against her grave.

"Why?"

Patrick stared at his feet and took a deep breath before answering. "Because I lost her too. I lost both of you that night."

Madison's eyes narrowed. "Are you kidding me?" She turned abruptly and began walking back to her car.

"Maddie, wait!"

"Don't call me that!" she barked, not turning around.

"Madison, please! Stop! We need to talk!"

"No, we don't!" she shouted over her shoulder as she continued to walk quickly to her car. "Why do you think I haven't returned any of your calls or emails, Patrick? Because there's nothing left to talk about!"

Patrick caught up to Madison, grabbed her arm and spun her around. "But we do. I miss you."

"I don't care anymore. And don't ever grab me like that again," Madison snapped, ripping her arm out of his hand.

Chapter Twelve

Madison couldn't shake the anger she felt from her encounter with Patrick the entire drive back to Meaford. What made her angrier was the nerve he had showing up at Annie's grave and trying to talk to her after she had clearly been ignoring him.

A couple times on the drive, Jules had tried calling Madison like she said she would but, after running into Patrick, Madison wasn't in the right state to talk to her about what had happened with Jake that morning. Besides, she figured it would be better if she talked to Jake first about what had happened than his sister – even if she was Madison's only friend up north.

By the time she reached the cottage, she was emotionally drained and decided that she had wasted enough energy fussing over Patrick and instead would focus more on the present and the future; and that meant fixing things with Jake.

Madison arrived at Middleton the next morning at her usual early time and was relieved to see Jake's truck was also in the parking lot. Madison wanted to use the time they had alone before everyone else arrived as an opportunity for her to apologize and for them to talk about what happened. However, when she walked into the barn Jake wasn't in there and everything was already set-up. When she walked into the lunchroom her heart sank because he wasn't in there either and all of the jobs were already written on the chalkboard. It was clear to Madison that Jake was purposefully avoiding her because he was already out on the course.

Madison took a closer look at the board and skimmed the employee list of names for hers. She was cutting greens with Robbie and Oskar in the morning and mowing fairways with Ben once that was done. Madison couldn't help but think Jake had also purposefully put Ben with Madison to cut fairways rather than Jules because he didn't want her and Jules to have a chance to talk. Although she knew he was mad, Madison had a hard time not thinking he was being a bit childish: first avoiding her in the morning and now for having her cut fairways with someone other than Jules.

She looked beside Jake's name and saw that he was working on an irrigation leak at the driving range for the day. When these were hers and Jake's jobs, that usually meant Jake and Madison went the whole day without seeing one another and, again, Madison couldn't help but think that it had been done on purpose.

She knew they needed to talk and the only reason she didn't try to last night was because she thought the extra time apart to think things over would benefit both of them. Now, going out of her way to see him on the driving range during the day seemed unprofessional and just a bad idea.

Before her co-workers began to arrive, Madison decided to head out in her golf cart with her trailer and walker in tow to the putting greens and begin cutting. While she didn't have to, because work didn't officially start for another half hour, Madison not only didn't feel like sitting around waiting for work to start but talking to everyone as they arrived about how fun the wedding had been sounded terrible.

It was still slightly dark outside when she left the maintenance shop, but the golf cart and walker mower both had lights, and by the time she got out there and was set-up she would only have to do a few passes with the lights.

All morning, Madison had tried to act as if nothing was bothering her, but her mind was elsewhere. She constantly went over the potential conversations and scenarios her and Jake were bound to have, and regardless of how they went, she always felt bad. As the day wore on, the more she became absolutely certain that she needed to talk to Jake as soon as the workday was over, but not just about Becca and Mike, about Patrick too. She hadn't conscientiously lied to Jake about Patrick, she just had chosen to leave him out of her story.

While Madison was putting her fairway mower's buckets back on the machine after washing them, in the distance she could hear the Kubota that Jake usually drove approaching. Madison stopped working and stood to the side of her machine in the hopes that he'd see her and pull over to at least say hello. It wasn't much, but just having some contact with him, even if it was just a hello, would help put her mind at ease. Instead, he roared passed Madison, not even looking at her. She stared at him in disbelief as he drove by and screeched to a halt by the maintenance shop's side door. Just as he was about to get out of the Kubota, a car pulled into the parking lot, and stopped beside him.

She didn't recognize the car as anyone's that worked at Middleton, but when the driver got out and shook Jake's hand, Madison's heart stopped.

Without so much as nodding hello, Jake decided to drive by Madison at the wash bay. He knew her and Ben would be there cleaning their fairway units, but he was still angry about what had happened at the wedding and Sunday morning, that he still didn't know exactly what to say to Madison. Plus, Ben was right beside her washing his machine and Jake needed to be professional while at work.

Although separating Madison and Jules while assigning jobs that morning hadn't been his finest moment, he was still hurt and trying to figure out why Madison hadn't just told him the truth about her run in with Becca – especially when she knew the history, he had with her. Even though she made it seem like she was going to tell him about it Sunday morning, he still felt like he had been lied to, and Madison knew that lying was a huge part of why him and Becca broke up. So why had she kept something as big as that from him?

Jake was about to start his end of day tasks around the shop when an unfamiliar car pulled into the maintenance parking lot. It had surprised Jake and he screeched the Kubota to a halt beside the side maintenance door louder than he had anticipated.

"Can I help you?" Jake asked across the Kubota bench to the man through his unrolled passenger window.

The man got out of the car and walked over to the side of the vehicle. Outstretching his arm, he shook Jake's hand, "I hope so. I'm looking for Maddie."

"Do you mean Madison?" Jake asked tentatively. He took a second glance at the man's car and saw what looked like a bouquet of flowers on its passenger seat.

The man smirked and looked around. Spotting her at the wash pad, he replied, "Sure, but I see she's right there."

"And you are?" Jake asked.

"Patrick. Her boyfriend."

Jake tilted his head and leaned in closer to him. "Excuse me?"

Patrick looked back towards the wash bay and gave a quick wave to Madison. "You must be Jake."

Jake let out an exacerbated sigh, "Oh, you know about me?"

"Oh yeah," he replied smiling at Madison as she began to run towards them. "I think I may have surprised her; I don't think she was expecting me," Patrick smugly said.

"Her and me both," Jake scoffed as he pressed down on the pedal of the Kubota and drove off.

"What are you doing here? How did you *even* find me?" Madison demanded. The moment she realized who Jake was shaking hands with, she dropped the last fairway bucket from her hands and began running towards them. Fuming at Patrick, she was now standing where Jake's Kubota had just been.

"Hi, again."

"*How* did you find me?"

"We need to talk."

"No, you need to answer my question."

"Well, you wouldn't hear me out yesterday...."

She folded her arms across her chest. "You're still not answering my question."

"...And your dad nearly punched me when I went by their house looking for you...." Realizing his charm wasn't working in dissuading Madison's anger, Patrick swallowed hard. "I followed you yesterday."

"You *what*?"

"Now that I've said it out loud, it sounds way more stalkerish then I intended it to be, but you left me no other choice. Maddie-"

"Stop calling me that."

"What?"

"That was Annie's nickname for me, not yours."

"It wasn't *anyone's* nickname, we both called you that...."

"No. Annie had called me that since we were babies, you just started calling me that after our first year of dating. So it wasn't yours to begin with and since we're not together anymore, you don't get to call me that."

"How can you say we're not together anymore?" he asked quietly.

"Pretty easily actually."

"So, this is how you're going to end our three years together?"

"No, no, you ended those three years a few months ago by your words, I just finalized it by breaking up with you afterwards."

"Maddie - Madison, come on. That's not fair; I was drunk."

Madison snorted. "I'm not having this conversation again with you here. Or anywhere for that matter. I'm at work and I moved to get away from you and everything else, so go home."

"No, not until we talk. Have dinner with me tonight and allow me to explain."

"No."

"Please."

"No!"

"I won't leave until you say yes." He placed his hand on her shoulder more gently than yesterday's grab. "We can work through this."

She looked at him appallingly before tearing away from his hand. "No, we can't and we won't. I said everything I needed to say to you the night we broke up. Go home and leave me alone, you've ruined things enough." Madison stepped away and opened the maintenance door but paused halfway through it. Turning back to face him, she said, "And don't ever follow me again."

Inside the maintenance shop, Madison headed straight for the bathroom. Locking its door, she put the toilet lid down and sat with her head in her hands.

After a few moments, there was a light knock on the door. "Madison? Are you okay? Who was that guy?" Jules asked.

So many answers to Jules's question rolled through her mind, but now wasn't the time to answer them or explain because she needed to find Jake.

Madison wiped the tears from her cheeks and opened the bathroom door. "No one important, but I need to find Jake. Do you know where he went in the Kubota?"

"He's not in the Kubota anymore. He just got in his truck and left for the day," Jules replied.

"To go home?"

Jules shook her head.

"Jules, I really need to talk to him. I'm pretty sure that guy that was out there just made things a lot worse between Jake and I. Where is he?"

"At the hospital. Visiting Becca."

Meaford's hospital was small so Jake knew exactly where Becca's room would be and simply walked past the reception desk as he entered the hospital. Not to mention that Becca had been admitted for overdosing at least two times when they were together, so needless to say he knew the hospital quite well.

Jake slowed as he neared the corner of the hallway that would lead to where Becca's room was. He knew there was a good chance that Mike would be around, and Jake wanted to know exactly what he was walking into. Peering carefully around the corner, Jake saw Mike sitting with his father, Tom, outside of a hospital room that he assumed would be Becca's. Mike was chewing on his fingers while his knees bounced up and down so fast that it looked like *he* was on cocaine.

Here we go, Jake thought and walked around the corner.

Sensing new movement, Mike instantly looked up, but had to do a double take before he realized who was walking towards them. "Oh, you've got to be kidding me," he said getting up angrily.

Jake stopped where he was and threw his arms in the air defensively. "I've just come to see how Becca's doing."

Mike was standing inches from Jake's face within seconds. "What, cuz' you suddenly care about her now? It takes Becca being in the hospital for you to give a-"

"That's enough, Michael," Tom said behind him. He placed a hand on Mike's shoulder and softly steered him back in the direction of their seats. "Hello, Jake," he said stretching his hand out for Jake to shake.

The scene of Tom and Jake shaking hands may have seemed like not a lot to someone passing by, but shaking Tom's hand was the most civilized thing that had happened between Jake and Becca's family since he ended their engagement.

"You can't be serious." Mike seethed beside his father.

"We've blamed him enough for something he tried to get us to see. You heard the doctor, Michael. Becca wouldn't have survived that car accident if she hadn't been strung out on cocaine. Jake told us she was addicted and that she needed help well over a year ago now."

Mike's face reddened. "Yeah, and he's the guy to blame for getting her hooked-on cocaine in the first place!"

Tom sighed heavily. "Stop it. You know he's not."

"So just like that." Mike snapped his fingers. "He's off the hook for all of Becca's problems? Unbelievable." He shrugged his father's hand off his shoulder before furiously walking down the hall. "You better not be here when I get back!" he said yelling back to Jake.

"He'll come around," Tom said quietly. "Heather's just gone home to get a few things, but if she were here, she would want to apologize with me for how we've mistreated you. How *all* of us have mistreated you. We were ignorant to our own little girl's problems and couldn't see them for what they were, even when you told us. Whatever happened at that wedding was, obviously, not your fault or your friend's. Becca arrived high and drunk and left higher and drunker. They found traces of cocaine, meth, alcohol, and a whole other assortment of things in her system. And she was certainly not re-invited to the wedding like she lied to Michael." Tom crossed his arms on his chest and brought his right hand to his face as he tried to hold back his tears. "I just don't know how we didn't believe you. All the signs were there. None of this would be happening right now if we'd just believed you when you tried helping her in the first place."

Even before their engagement ended, Jake had realized and come to terms with the fact that his once almost in-laws, who at one point adored him, didn't believe a word he told them about Becca's drug problem. To be fair, their son, Mike, always provided the counter argument that Becca wasn't addicted to cocaine every time Jake tried to tell them that she was, so Tom and Heather were put in a tough position of believing their son or their future son-in-law. It took Jake a long time, a lot of sleepless nights, and a lot of long conversations with his dad, Scott and Jules, for him to recover from the feeling of betrayal their disbelief in him led to, so to hear Tom apologize was surreal. And in that moment, the weight of the blame and guilt Jake had felt because of everything that had happened with Becca was lifted from his shoulders.

"How's she doing?" Jake asked, trying not to sound too emotional.

"She woke up." Tom half smiled. "But she's sleeping most of the time and usually has a really bad headache. They have her on antidepressants because she's also in withdrawal and there's a counsellor coming to see her sometime this week." Tom's voice cracked.

"Becca will pull through. She's a fighter."

Tom sniffled a couple of times before coughing and agreeing with Jake.

"Do you think I could see her?" Jake asked gently.

"Why would you want to? I don't mean to sound rude, but she's been awful to you."

"You're right, but the old Becca's still in there somewhere and that's who I want to see."

Tom merely nodded as tears silently rolled down his cheeks. He put his hand on Jake's shoulder. "She was lucky to have had you, Jake. We all were. Again, I'm so sorry for how we treated you."

Still in shock from how unreal Tom's words were, Jake only nodded as he made his way towards Becca's hospital room.

Tears instantly welled in his eyes when he opened the door and saw the woman he had almost married bruised and bandaged beyond recognition. Her left arm and leg were in casts, and she was hooked up to a ventilator, a catheter, and two IV lines. The only noises in her room were the beeping from machines and the ventilator rising and falling beside her bed.

Suddenly the urge for Becca to be able to hear something other than machines overtook him and he frantically searched for the remote control. Finding it, he switched the television on and found a rerun of FRIENDS playing on one of the channels.

Standing next to her bed, he rested his hand on its corner and a rush of some of their better memories together came flooding back. Jake felt his knees get weak and, thankfully, there was a chair behind him that he was able to stumble into. Suddenly, tears began to fall down his face and his head quickly began to feel heavy. Resting it in the palms of his hands he quietly sobbed.

Jake and Becca had gone to high school together, but Becca was two years older than him, so they knew of each other but didn't really know one another. Then, when Jake had been accepted to Guelph for their Associate Diploma in Turf Grass Management program, he looked for a carpooling buddy to drive back to Meaford with on weekends and someone had mentioned Becca's name. She had taken the two years that he was finishing high school to backpack through Europe and Asia and was also just starting her first year, but for veterinarian services.

Jake had been captivated by her and her stories from their very first carpool ride, and he became infatuated with her just as fast. Within a couple of weeks, he asked her out, and they officially began dating not too long after that. Pretty quickly after they started dating, he caught the travel bug from her and throughout their almost five years of being together they had backpacked Argentina, Norway and eastern Europe together while also doing smaller trips within North America. Jake proposed to her after they'd completed a goal of theirs while in Norway: surfing and skiing in the same day. Despite Becca's denials later when he asked if she was high when he'd proposed, as time wore on Jake felt confident that she was.

A couple of months before they went to Norway, Becca went to an all-inclusive resort with some new friends she had met at a party. But from the moment Jake had met those friends, he knew he didn't like them. He couldn't see what Becca saw in them and thought they were nothing but trouble. Turns out they were because they were the ones that not only got her hooked-on cocaine but were also her supplier. Not to mention a whole other slew of drugs they got her to try, too.

Becca had started acting differently and Jake attributed it to finals and wedding planning, but then he caught her doing a line of coke in his bedroom one morning right after she'd woken up. They'd gotten into their first major fight, but Becca had assured him she was just going through a phase because she was so stressed, and that the cocaine helped her relax. Then, Jake caught her doing another line in his bathroom a month later and right before they were supposed to go to her parents for dinner. They got into an even bigger fight and, hoping it would deter her from using, he asked her never to bring cocaine into his house again. However, that didn't stop her because she just did lines of coke before going over or would make an excuse to go for random walks and do the lines outside before she stopped going over entirely. It was then that Jake finally realized that

Becca had been addicted and was using way more than she was letting on.

Becca changed drastically; she began to hide stuff from him, lie about petty things, stay out all hours during the week and on weekends, not show up for work, and stopped wearing her engagement ring most days. Becca quickly became someone completely different than the woman he had fallen in love with, and someone he didn't want to spend the rest of his life with.

However, none of that seemed to matter anymore as he sat across from her in her hospital room while she lay next to him fighting for her life. In spite of the many nights of Jules, their father, and Scott being his sounding boards, and the hours they spent helping him realize that what Becca had done, and was still doing, wasn't his fault, Jake still felt like there was more he could have done. More he *should* have done. And in that moment, all that shame came flooding back.

Jake pulled the chair closer to her bed and gently took Becca's hand in his. Resting her hand on his cheek, he whispered, "What have you been doing, Bec? What happened to you? To us?"

Jake waited for a response that he knew wasn't coming. Instead, he got the machines' beeping, the ventilator rising and falling, and Chandler Bing making a joke.

When Jake first broke their engagement off, he regularly dreamed that Becca would get sober and that they would get back together. But, over time, that desire had gone away, and his feelings for her became less and less. But here and now, the desire for the old Becca to come back to him was stronger than ever.

Chapter Thirteen

Madison stopped washing the dishes when she heard a car pull into the driveway. She rested her hands on the sink's rim, letting the soapy water drip off them. She really hoped it was Jake, but a small fear ran through her that it could be Mike again.

All evening she had wanted to stop by Jake's house, or at the very least call him, especially because of whatever had transpired between him and Patrick, but she felt hurt he'd gone to visit Becca. Madison knew she shouldn't because Jake had every right to visit whoever he wanted, but it was everything else that surrounded him visiting her in the hospital that hurt. In addition to him purposefully avoiding her at work, would he have visited Becca if they weren't arguing or if Patrick hadn't stopped by and said whatever he did that made Jake leave work in such a haste? What did this mean for her and Jake? Was there even a 'her and Jake' to worry about anymore?

Madison dried her hands on a tea towel and quietly stepped into the bathroom to see out its window. "You've got to be kidding me," she mumbled angrily walking into the hallway. "I thought I told you not to follow me again?" Madison called through the closed front door.

Patrick stood on the other side with a bouquet of flowers and a brown paper bag. "I'm sorry for following you yesterday and blindsiding you at work earlier."

"And for following me here?"

"I didn't follow you here, I've been driving around every street in town looking for your car."

"That seems a bit excessive when I distinctly told you to leave me alone."

"Well, I was going crazy just waiting in the motel room-"

"Wait, wait, wait. Motel room?"

"Madison, I really want to talk to you and to try and figure this out...."

She snarled, "You are unbelievable!"

"...Call it lucky because this was the last road I was going to drive down tonight before heading back. This Chinese food's pretty cold by now, though." There was an awkward pause that she knew he was hoping for her to cave and say something, but she remained silent. Clearing his throat, he continued, "Look, I just want to know how you're doing and to apologize, and when you wouldn't return my calls, emails or texts, and then I saw you yesterday, it just felt like an opportunity."

Madison remained quiet for several minutes and hoped he would clue in and get the picture that she didn't want him there and just leave, but instead she heard him take a seat on one of the porch steps.

"I quit drinking," he said quietly. "For good this time. I'm getting more help than before, I even joined AA."

Madison's tone softened a little. "Good for you, Patrick. But how do you see this playing out? You treated me so poorly when Annie died and when I needed you the most, not to mention everything I put up with before. Did you really think you'd come find me, fix everything between us, and then I'd come home?"

"I really screwed up, okay? But I was drunk-"

"So that makes what you said okay?" she asked getting angry again.

"No, but-"

"But nothing! That's not an excuse and how dare you try to use it as one! But it's not just that, when I really needed you because my best friend died beside me, you should have been there for me, comforting me, telling me that everything was going to be okay, but you weren't. And then you had the audacity to ask me if *I* had been drunk when I was driving Annie home from the party, basically accusing me of killing my best friend!"

"You're right. I've been an awful boyfriend. Before and after Annie passed. But why didn't you wait for me to sober up so I could apologize and explain?"

Madison laughed mockingly. "You're kidding, right? Do you even realize what just came out of your mouth?"

"Well, I want to know why you just left like that."

"I didn't just leave, Patrick; I broke up with you."

A few moments passed when neither one of them said anything, but Madison was pretty sure she could hear him crying.

"I was hoping that by coming up here we could talk things through…."

"Why? So, *you* can say sorry, so *you* feel better about how you treated me? Seriously, think about why you're really here. Is it to make me feel better or to make yourself feel better because it sure feels like it's the latter!"

"I guess if we're being so honest-"

"Please! For once!"

"…a little bit of both. Can we please just share this cold Chinese food together and talk inside? Or out here, just not with a door between us."

Madison took a deep breath before she opened the front door. Patrick quickly wiped his eyes with the sleeves of his shirt and stood up.

"Hi."

"You can come in under a couple conditions."

"Okay."

"We are not getting back together, and we are just talking. That's it, okay?"

When Patrick nodded, Madison stepped back into the cottage. Leaving the front door open, he followed behind her.

"Whatever you have to say better be damn good," she said before taking a seat at the kitchen table.

Patrick placed the flowers and the bag of Chinese food on the buffet. "Oh, you already have flowers," he said sounding bitter and pointing to the ones on the table beside her that Jake had brought before the wedding.

"If you're going to talk about the flowers that I already have, then get out."

He sighed. "You've changed."

"That's what death and betrayal can do to a person," Madison replied firmly. "But I also just learned not to take shit anymore."

He closed his eyes and looked genuinely hurt. "Do you have another vase?"

"You do realize that you haven't changed though, right? You're still trying to be beat around the bush and stall; trying to bide time with your charm for me to calm down and say that everything's fine." She shook her head in disbelief. "Don't worry about putting the flowers in a vase, Patrick. Tell me something, how long did it take you to figure out that I'd actually broken up with you?"

He avoided her eyes for a minute before finally answering. "I blacked out that night, so I don't really remember much," he mumbled.

"And what about the night you accused me of being drunk and driving Annie home?"

"I didn't accuse you; it was just a stupid thing I said."

"If you think your comment was just 'something stupid' then you really have no clue how hurtful what you said was, and that you actually are here just for yourself."

"I screwed up, Madison. Again. And I'm sorry. I shouldn't have said-"

"You know what you said that night was just my breaking point, right? Everything else, all our previous problems up until that point had just been the gravy. To be honest, I should have broken up with you a long time ago, Annie certainly wanted me to. But when I was in the hospital after the car accident, the *same* one that killed Annie, you were barely there. Yet somehow you were still able to drink with your buddies."

Patrick bowed his head. "I was there for a bit, but I was drunk when I found out you were in the hospital. Then when I left, the guys wanted to help me take my mind off everything, so they took me out...."

"But that's just it, Patrick. My parents said you left the hospital after, like, thirty minutes. We'd been together three years and you didn't think to stay a little longer with me? Or maybe to sober up and come back?"

"I had to go home to shower. I was hungover and I needed to wake up a bit more."

"But then you should have come back!" she yelled at him jumping out of her chair. "You *should* have come back!"

"I know! I realize all of this now which is why I'm here. I need you to know how sorry I am and I need you to tell me how to make things right between us."

"There is no 'us' anymore."

"So that's it?"

Madison nodded. "Yes, Patrick. That's it."

He leaned back against the kitchen counter and folded his arms. "So, what happens now?"

"What do you mean? You go home, and I stay here."

"Madison, I don't think that's how this should end."

She stared at him disbelievingly. He may have claimed to have stopped drinking, but it was like he was drunk because nothing she said was getting through to him. "You know, it's taken me a long time to realize just how incredibly selfish you are. Have you not listened to a word I've said? This has already ended because I already decided how it ends."

"I know I've been the worst person and that you deserve more, so here I am trying to be better."

"To make *you* feel better."

"No, Madison. I know there are no words that will ever express to you how truly sorry I am for the crap I put you through or for awful I was when you were in the hospital and Annie died. But that's why I'm here; actions speak louder than words."

Madison stared confusedly at him. "Really? Don't you think that sounds a bit ironic coming from you?"

"Yeah, but it's the truth."

"Is this all what you've been wanting to say to me over these last few months?" Madison asked.

"I guess so."

They stood wordlessly for a few moments, the air around them heavy with hurt.

Patrick coughed. "Your dad, um, nearly broke my nose when I went to their house looking for you. It was a few days after you wouldn't return any of my messages."

"What?" she asked stunned.

"Yeah, he obviously didn't appreciate how I treated you either. Your mom held him back, but then she almost came at me herself. I kind of wish she'd hit me, or at least one of them did."

Madison couldn't help but laugh at the thought of her parents punching him in the face.

"Oh, you think that's funny, do you?" Patrick asked, laughing himself. "I don't deserve a lot, but I do deserve a good punch in the face. Speaking of which, I'm a bit surprised that guy Jake didn't punch me earlier."

"What did you say to him?"

Patrick took a deep breath. "I told him I was your boyfriend."

No wonder Jake hadn't stopped by or tried to call her. "Come on, Patrick! What's wrong with you? Why would you do that?"

"I was hoping I still had a chance."

She looked at him with scorn. "You really are the most ignorant and unobservant person I've ever met."

"I'm sorry that I lied to him."

Madison took a deep breath. "I really wish you hadn't come. Not only because I'd given no indication that I ever wanted to see you again, but also because there's a lot going on right now, besides trying to deal with Annie's death and, honestly, you've only made it worse."

"I hope he treats you better than I did...."

"Wow, did you really not hear anything I just said?"

"It's fine, really. I can accept when I know I've been replaced-"

"Replaced? A minute ago, you were trying to get back together with me and now you're saying you're okay with me moving on, and are trying to get information out of me about that relationship? This isn't going anywhere and we're just going in circles, so this conversation's over and you should go."

He threw his hands up defensively. "Okay, replaced may not have been the best word to use, but look, I'm just trying to find out if you're doing alright. You're up here all alone."

"I'm not alone, but we're still done here, and you need to go. And take the flowers and food with you; I already ate, and I already have flowers." She opened the front door and stood beside it. "Goodbye Patrick."

Chapter Fourteen

Jake let out an exasperated sigh when he saw both Jules and Scott's cars in his driveway. He knew they would want to talk to him about what was going on and, despite trying to avoid that by having driven around aimlessly for hours after his hospital visit, they were still there. He'd hoped that if he had come home late enough, they would have just decided to go to Jules's place, but clearly, they hadn't.

When he walked into the main room, Jules was sitting on the couch reading a magazine.

She smiled. "Hey. Scott's out for a run."

"Hi. Just so we're clear, I don't feel like talking."

"What? I'm just sitting here...." she said innocently.

"Okay," he said walking past her, heading straight for the bathroom.

Jake knew his sister well enough that he knew she wasn't 'just sitting' there but instead had been patiently waiting all day for him to come home. He knew Jules meant it in a supportive way, she always did, but sometimes he just needed to figure things out for himself.

Hopping into the shower, he hoped that he would feel better after washing the day away, but his mind just kept wandering. What was going on? Did Madison really have a boyfriend and had she had one this whole time? Was his almost future wife seriously laying in a hospital bed clinging to life? Did she only survive a horrific accident because she was high on the same drug that tore them apart? Had Tom really just apologized?

Taking longer than his normal three-minute shower, Jake let the hot water beat against his skin as his mind searched for answers. When he finally turned off the water, Jake felt somewhat refreshed but still hadn't gained any insight into the whirlwind of questions that were churning around in his head.

He changed into black workout shorts and a dark blue dry fit t-shirt and planned to spend the rest of the night reading in his room, until his stomach growled. Great, he thought. His plan to avoid Jules was foiled because to make food he'd have to face her. Jake loved that his sister was dating Scott for many reasons, one of which was that it meant he got to see her even more than he did before, but in this very moment he wished that they weren't so he could be home alone.

When he walked out of his room, Jules was sitting on the couch in the same spot she had been when he got home. Walking past her into the kitchen, he could feel her eyes on him. He stood staring into the fridge, examining the groceries Scott had picked up earlier in the day for them and tried to piece together what he was going to make for dinner. As much as he didn't want to talk to Jules, because he knew as soon as he said one thing she would use it as a segue to start a conversation about what was going on, he wasn't about to make dinner for himself in front of her.

He exhaled deeply, "Have you eaten?"

Jules immediately slammed the magazine shut and threw it on the coffee table. She jumped up from the couch and headed straight to the breakfast buffet chairs. "Yes, but thank you for asking. If I may…." she began.

"Nope," Jake said, pulling trout out of the fridge. "I already told you that I don't feel like talking."

Ignoring him, she continued. "Why did you visit Becca?"

He opened the spice cupboard and pulled out the Cajun seasoning. "Not happening, Jules."

"Jake, you've come so far."

"Jules, stop."

"Okay. Fine. What's going on with Madison then?"

"I also don't feel like talking about her."

"Jake-"

He stopped his food prep and rested his hands on the counter. "Look, it's been a weird couple of days, and I'm angry, and I'm hurt, and I just don't want to talk about it with anyone. It's not personal, okay?"

Jules hesitated at the buffet before she reluctantly walked back over to the couch and picked up the magazine again.

After spreading the seasoning over top of the trout, Jake put it aside and began chopping broccoli.

A few minutes passed before Scott came home from his run. He nodded a silent hello to Jake before kissing Jules on the cheek and then headed into the bathroom to have a shower.

"See, he gets it," Jake said cheekily once he'd heard the water turn on.

Jules shot up from the couch again, "Well, if you're going to be sassy then I'm not going to listen to you. You need to go talk to Madison and hear her out."

"No, I don't think I do. Besides, her boyfriend's in town so if she needs someone to talk to, she can talk to him."

"Um, I'm fairly certain there's more to that situation than you think."

"Oh? And why do you think that?"

"Because she came flying into the shop just after you left and locked herself in the bathroom. It was pretty clear that she was really upset-"

"Well I would be too if I'd been trying to get with someone all summer only to have my partner show up unexpectedly and ruin everything!" He snapped. "He sounded pretty confident when he told me he was her boyfriend."

"And you believe a guy you just met over Madison? When she came out of the bathroom all she could think about was finding you so you guys could talk. She wanted nothing to do with that guy and didn't care that he was there at all! She just wanted to find you...until I told her where you were."

"So, she knows?" he asked.

"What, were you going to keep that from her?"

"Like how she talked to Becca at the wedding and kept that from me? Or how she's had a boyfriend all summer and kept that from me? It seems only fitting that I keep some things from her, too!"

"Don't be stupid, Jake."

Even as he said the last part, he knew it sounded ridiculous and he didn't mean it. He would have told Madison he had visited Becca in the hospital when they saw each other next. He hated lying and dishonesty and thought she did, too.

"Things aren't always what they seem," Jules said softly. "Just imagine how Madison's feeling right now."

He slammed the knife he was using down and angrily shouted, "Imagine how Madison feels right now? Are you joking me?"

"No, I'm not! You're falling back into the whole 'Becca's the victim' thing again. We worked *so* hard to help you get out of that, and you were. And then Madison came, and you guys hit it off and it was obvious to everyone that you guys were falling in love. But then Becca got her little crazy fingers in on yours and Madison's relationship. So, Madison needed a little time to process whatever the hell Becca said to her at the wedding? She's probably never had to deal with a psycho before! And now Becca's won all over again because as soon as things got a little difficult with Madison you ran straight back to Becca. You're spiraling, Jake! So yeah, imagine how Madison's feeling."

"I'm sorry all of yours and everyone's hard work has gone to waste," Jake said defiantly.

Jules and Jake stared at each other heatedly before Scott walked back into the living room. "Can you and my sister go for a walk or something, please?" Jake asked.

"No, not until you tell us why you went and visited Becca."

Jake rolled his eyes. "Really? You too? Thanks for your support, man."

"I'm sorry, Jake, but Jules is right."

"Is Jules right because she's my sister or is she right because she's your girlfriend?" As soon as the words came out of his mouth, he regretted them.

Scott being Scott ignored his comment and continued. "So, Becca got into an accident? It sucks, but it was bound to happen, you must know that. She's been addicted to cocaine and who knows what else for a really long time. I mean, really, who's to say she didn't do it on purpose to try and get your attention? Nothing else she was doing was working."

"Becca wouldn't do that!" Jake yelled.

"Maybe not the old Becca, but she's gone, man!" Scott shouted right back. "She's been gone a long time."

Jules' voice softened. "I get that things are crazy right now and your emotions are all over the place, but what we're saying isn't shocking, Jake, you already know all of this about Becca. I also get that it's hard to remember the bad things when someone you cared for is in the hospital, we just don't want you to forget everything she's put you through because she was in an accident. And on top of that, the hurt you're feeling from what you think is going on with Madison and-"

"Wouldn't you be hurt?"

"Of course, but you don't know the full story. You could be feeling upset right now over nothing because you haven't talked to Madison. You only know what you think you know from what that guy said. Don't lose what you have with Madison over miscommunication."

"Even if he's not her boyfriend, they clearly have a history together, so why would she have kept that from me all summer? I thought we had been completely open with one another and now who's to say what else she's been keeping from me? This situation seems oddly familiar, and I'm *not* going down that road again."

"Go and talk to Madison. Don't punish her for something Becca did to you."

He shook his head while wiping his hands on a tea towel. "I'll clean this up later. I'm going out for a drive."

"Jake-"

"Don't follow me," he interrupted her and slammed the porch door behind him.

Jake jumped in his truck and began unconsciously driving in the direction of his favourite look-out; the same one he had brought Madison to before they went to Leeky Canoe a few months ago. Even though he wanted to be alone because he needed to think, a small part of him thought Madison would be there. The lookout wasn't far from his house, and within five minutes he was pulling into its empty parking lot.

The sun had begun its descent and as it slowly disappeared, purple and pink splashed across the sky in its place. Sunsets in Meaford had always been stunning and their natural beauty was something that could always help calm Jake and clear his head. He turned his truck off and sat staring at the sky overlooking Georgian Bay.

Jake was angry with Madison, but most of all he was hurt. Despite what he thought were raw and genuine moments that they had had, she conscientiously chose not to tell him about her conversation with Becca and that guy claiming to be her boyfriend. Now that he was thinking about it, she hadn't mentioned anything about any past relationships at all which he now thought was even more suspicious. Madison knew practically everything there was to know about him, but there were still so many question marks around her.

Maybe Jake had become a sucker for damsels in distress? Maybe he saw the hurt in her eyes from losing Annie when they first met, and he recognized the same hurt he'd had in his eyes after he lost his mom? Or maybe Madison was just more like Becca than he initially thought?

Taking a deep breath, he shook his head knowing that his last thought wasn't true. It was just that Madison's words and actions didn't add up and that was one of the most hurtful and frustrating parts.

Something in the back of his mind nagged at him, though, and he could only assume it was something that Jules had said. As much as he didn't like to admit it, Jules was usually right about most things. Although she was a year younger, ever since their mom had died, she had slowly transitioned from younger sister to a woman with a motherly air about her. Not in an overpowering or condescending way, but enough that it was as if Jules was sometimes, somehow, becoming their mother.

It finally dawned on him what it was that Jules had said that had been bugging him: 'Don't lose what you have over miscommunication.'

"Fine," Jake said turning his truck back on and reversing out of the parking lot.

Madison's cottage wasn't far from the lookout, but throughout the short drive he couldn't help but think that he should have just gone over to her house sooner so all of this could have been cleared up.

When he pulled onto her road, his hands became clammy, and his heart began to beat faster. What if it wasn't a big misunderstanding and she had been playing him this whole time? If that were the case, was he prepared to accept that? No, he adamantly thought, because it had to have been a big misunderstanding.

However, when his truck rounded the bend in the road and her cottage came into view, he hit the brakes. The same car that her alleged boyfriend was driving earlier was in her driveway.

He let out an annoyed grunt. "What?"

Jake's truck sat in the middle of the one lane road as he went over possible scenarios as to why that guy's car would be in Madison's driveway at this time of night, but wasn't having much luck.

After a few minutes passed, another car came up behind him. Dense bush lined the road her cottage was on meaning no two cars could pass at the same time; one of them would need to pull into a driveway to allow the other by. As Jake looked ahead, all the driveways to the cottages leading to Madison's were full and didn't have enough room for Jake to pull his truck in, so he took his foot off the brake and slowly approached Madison's place.

As he drove by, no one was in the car and the lights weren't on inside her cottage, so it was hard to see anything. The cottage to the left of hers was empty so Jake pulled into it to allow the car behind him to pass by.

Her neighbour's cottage sat higher than Madison's and was slightly closer to the water, meaning from their driveway someone could see into Madison's kitchen window.

As Jake started to reverse back out of the driveway and head home, something caught his eye through the window. There, resting on the buffet was the bouquet of flowers that he'd seen in the guy's car from earlier. It wasn't cold hard evidence of anything, but it was all Jake needed to see. He swallowed hard, finally accepting that he had been played.

Continuing to back his truck up, his cellphone rang. Slamming the transmission into drive, he answered his phone without looking at its caller I.D. "What?" He snapped.

"Jake? It's Tom Smith."

He hit the brakes. "Hi, Tom. Sorry."

"Becca's awake and she's asked to see you. I know it's a lot to ask and it's getting late, but she won't talk to anyone else. Do you mind coming back to the hospital?"

"Of course. I'm on my way."

Jake rounded the hospital corner leading to Becca's room without hesitation this time and was relieved to only see Tom and Heather sitting outside of it. He doubted Mike would ever leave him alone, but he really wasn't in the mood to have to put up with him right now. Becca's parents stood when they saw him, and Heather approached him first.

"Thank you for coming again; I know you didn't have to."

"Is everything alright?"

"We think so, but when she woke up, she only asked for you and hasn't spoken since…."

The silence between the three of them grew heavy.

Here we go again, Jake thought.

"We know you don't have to do this, and we completely understand if you change your mind." Tom offered.

"Is anyone in there with her now?" Jake asked, pointing to the closed door and shut blinds.

"No, those are closed to stop light going in from the hallway. The light in the room is off to help with her concussion, but there's a small lamp in the corner that's on," Tom said.

Jake nodded slowly. As he had driven to the hospital, he thought about some of the things Jules and Scott had brought up earlier and accepted that, again, they had been right. He knew that if him and Becca were going to talk, it had to be on his terms. "If I go in there, I'd like to leave the door open a bit so you guys can hear what's being said and what's going on."

"Of course," Heather said.

"I can't promise anything because I have no idea what she wants, but I think you both know where I stand."

Tom put his arm around Heather's shoulder, and they nodded.

Jake took a deep breath before opening Becca's hospital door.

Even though there was a corner lamp on, it was set on dim leaving the room almost in complete darkness. As his eyes adjusted and he was able to make out her awake body, tears began to well in his eyes. "Bec-"

She half smiled and said in a raspy voice, "Thank you for coming. I know you didn't have to. I really messed up this time, didn't I?"

He nodded knowing that if he tried to speak, he might not be able to contain his emotions and he knew he needed to keep them in check.

"I'm so sorry, Jake, I don't even know where to begin...."

He looked down at his shoes. Did she really just apologize? First her father and now her? Was it genuine or was she just saying sorry because she knew he wanted to hear it? Three days ago, Jake would never have imagined he would ever hear her apologize but now.... He stepped closer to her bed, but abruptly stopped when she twitched.

"It's an effect from coming off the drugs," she explained.

Despite her present state, she sounded more like the old Becca than ever before, and Jake couldn't help but let out a small laugh of happiness at hearing her.

Tears fell down Becca's cheeks now, yet a smile spread across her face. "I'm back, Jake. I'm going to go get help. Counsellors are coming in later this week and I'll be going to rehab once I'm able to leave. It'll be a process, but I'm back. I promise."

He sat in the chair he'd sat in earlier in the day. "Bec-"

She tried to adjust how she was sitting but pain shot across her face. "No, Jake, listen. This accident was the best thing that could have happened to me – besides you, of course. There's no more hiding my problem, everyone knows. I'm just lucky that no one else was hurt. There are a lot of things I should have done differently, but I can't take those back. But I promise you that things will be different this time."

Jake pulled the chair closer to her bed and gently took her hand into his.

She began to sob, "You were so good to me even when I was the worst person to you. Please let me make it up to you and make up for the time that we've lost. I swear I'll be better than before."

Jake couldn't stop the few tears that fell down his cheeks, but he quickly wiped his eyes with his free hand. "I never wanted you to leave."

"I know, but I'm here now." Twitch.

He took a deep breath. "If only you'd come back sooner," he said, slowly pulling his hand away from hers. Sitting back in the chair, he ran his hands over his face.

"I'm here now, Jake" Becca said slower and more firmly. "And I love you."

He stood up. "Don't say that."

"I miss you. I miss us."

Tom softly knocked on the door. "Is everything alright in here?"

"Everything's fine, dad!" Becca snapped.

Jake froze from the tone she'd used that he'd heard all too often when she was high and aggravated.

"Sorry," Becca quickly replied. "I'm still working through a few things."

Tom and Jake locked eyes and Jake gave a slight nod, indicating that everything was fine.

"Did you slash Madison's tires?" Jake asked once Tom was out of the doorframe.

"Yes," Becca whispered.

"How did you know that she was at my place and that was her car?"

"Let's talk about something else, Jake."

"No, I want to talk about this. How did you know?"

"I wasn't in the right frame of mind that night and I've done a lot of things I'm not proud of."

"So, you keep saying. Were you stalking me or something? Or her?" Jake pressed.

Becca swallowed hard but remained silent.

"What did you say to her at Drew and Evelyn's wedding?"

"Why? Are you in love with her or something?" Becca snapped again.

Both Tom and Heather appeared in the doorway this time.

"You know, by you avoiding answering or choosing not to say anything, *are* answers, Becca. I hope counselling and rehab go well for you. You deserve to get better."

"Jake don't," Becca pleaded as he headed towards the door.

Ignoring her, he looked at her parents and said softly, "If she asks for me again, please don't call."

"Jake!"

"Goodbye, Becca."

Chapter Fifteen

Madison wasn't quite sure when she told Patrick to leave how he was going to react and was thankful that he left without picking a fight. In her experience, when things didn't go his way in the past, Patrick could sometimes develop a temper. It hadn't always been like that, but when he started drinking more and more frequently, it seemed like the alcohol and anger went hand in hand. Another reason of many as to why they were better apart.

By the time Patrick had pulled out of her driveway and she had calmed down from their conversation, it was late. She checked her cell phone and hoped she would see a missed call or message from Jake, but she didn't, and when she tried calling him it went straight to his voicemail. Throwing her phone on the couch out of anger, she took a few deep breaths while shaking her head in annoyance. How had things gone from so great to so lousy so quickly? How could she make them right again? Could she even make them right?

Madison had no way of knowing where Jake stood in terms of Becca now that she was in the hospital. Did her accident change his feelings for Becca? Had it made him realize that he couldn't live without her?

So many questions bounced around in her head as she paced back and forth in her living room. Knowing there was only one way to find out the answers, she grabbed her car keys and a jacket and headed out the door.

When she pulled onto Jake's street, she saw that his truck wasn't in the driveway but both Jules and Scott's vehicles were. Madison hesitated about whether to stop and check to see if he wasn't home or to assume that if his truck wasn't there that meant he wasn't either. Both options felt like no-win situations because if she stopped and Jules answered, it could look like

Madison was running to his sister for help or trying to pry information out of her. On the other hand, if Madison just assumed Jake wasn't home because his truck wasn't in the driveway, but it turned out he actually was, she'd feel foolish. Eventually Madison decided that the latter was worse and when she saw that there were some lights on inside, she parked her car and got out.

The front door was open allowing the warm evening breeze to flow through the screen door. Heading up the porch steps, she could hear the faint noise of a movie playing inside. When she knocked, the movie paused and there was some rustling inside before Scott appeared in the hallway.

He smiled sympathetically at her as he opened the screen door. "Hey Madison."

"Madison?" She heard Jules shout from inside. Before waiting for confirmation, Jules bounded towards the front door. "Madison! Are you okay? What's going on?"

"I'm fine. Is Jake home?"

Jules and Scott looked at each other before shaking their heads.

Madison continued, "I tried calling him, but it went straight to his voicemail. Do you have any idea where he is? I'd really like to talk to him."

"No, we don't. When he came home earlier, we chatted a bit, but he didn't like what we had to say and got mad and left. We haven't seen or heard from him since…." Jules answered.

"Okay. When he gets home, could you tell him I stopped by, please?"

"Of course," Scott said.

"Do you want to come in and wait?" Jules offered.

"No, I don't think that'd be a good idea, but thank you. See you guys tomorrow at work."

Madison felt deflated as she got back into her car. She didn't even want to toy with the possibility that Jake could be at the hospital again, but if he wasn't home at this time of night, where else could he be? Suddenly, it dawned on her: the look-out. When Jake picked her up a couple months ago before they met Jules and Scott at Leeky, he brought her to a lookout and said it was where he went when he needed to think about things. With her heart pounding, she turned her car around and headed west.

The lookout wasn't far and within a few moments her heart sank as she pulled into its parking lot and saw it empty. She parked in one of the spots and checked her phone again to see if Jake had texted or called her back but there were no messages or missed calls.

Even though Madison didn't know where the hospital in Meaford was, curiosity began nagging at her. She'd seen the blue and white 'H' signs throughout town and knew that if she really wanted to find it and check if he was there, she could just follow the signs. After a few minutes of internally debating with herself, she decided that was exactly what she was going to do. At the very least if his truck wasn't there it would settle her nerves.

Meaford's hospital sat on top of a small hill overlooking Georgian Bay. It wasn't very big and had a small parking lot, so it only took a couple seconds before Madison spotted Jake's truck.

She pulled over to the side of the road and hit the brakes. Madison didn't even realize she was crying until her cheeks were soaked. Quickly wiping them dry, she checked her blind spot and drove home.

Madison knew she wouldn't be able to sleep when she got back, so she poured herself a glass of wine. Grabbing the blanket from the couch, she headed onto the back deck, draped it over her legs and curled into a Muskoka chair. Closing her eyes, she let her thoughts drift as she listened to the frogs and crickets around her.

She didn't know how long she had been sitting there when the sound of a car approaching made her come back to reality. Opening her eyes, she saw its headlights turn into what appeared to be her driveway. Madison had no idea who would be visiting her at this time of night other than two people she really didn't want to see. As she waited for any signs that could help her figure out who it was, Madison couldn't decide who she wanted to see less of: Patrick or Mike.

Through the open window behind her, Madison could hear a soft knock on her front door. Sitting motionless, she hoped that whoever it was would assume she'd gone to bed and leave. The back-deck lights were on but were dimmed so she doubted whoever it was would see their illumination and think to check the backyard. Even if they did see them on, it wasn't out of the ordinary because people left outside lights on throughout the night all the time.

A few moments of silence went by and Madison couldn't figure out where the person had gone as she hadn't heard a car door open and close or drive away. But by the time she did hear footsteps approaching along the side of the house she had no time to think about what to do.

"Hi," Jake said putting his hands into his pockets.

"Hi," she repeated, relief washing over her that it was him.

"Jules and Scott said you stopped by."

"I did. But, uh, it's fine now. It must be pretty late."

"Close to 11:00 PM."

"So, what are you doing here, Jake?"

A surprised look crossed over his face before he shrugged and turned to leave. "No idea."

"What was that look for?" Madison asked getting up from the chair and walking to the side of the deck.

He stopped walking. "I guess I just expected something different."

"You and me both," she mumbled.

Jake swung around. "Then why did you come by?"

"Because I wanted to talk."

"And now suddenly you don't?"

"No, because I don't think we need to anymore."

"And why not?"

"I know you went to the hospital this afternoon."

"So?"

"And again tonight."

He raised his eyebrows at her, clearly expecting more of an explanation.

"So?" she repeated. "I can put two and two together."

"And I know that guy from earlier today was here tonight." A complex expression crossed Madison's face before Jake continued. "Yeah, I dropped by earlier hoping we could talk, but saw that your boyfriend was here instead."

"Jake, Patrick is not my boyfriend and hasn't been for a while."

"Then why did he say he was earlier?"

"Because he's a jerk! I visited Annie's grave yesterday and he eavesdropped on me telling her about you and what happened at the wedding. He followed me up here hoping he could fix things and probably figured if he told you he was my boyfriend that it would ruin things between us."

Jake clenched his jaw before asking, "Did he fix things between you?"

Madison rolled her eyes. "No, and he's never going to be able to. What happened between Patrick and I is unfixable."

Jake slowly nodded. "Look, I don't know how long-ago you guys broke up, but you could have at least mentioned something to him about me. When he showed up like that and said he was your boyfriend, it felt like the wool had been pulled over my eyes again."

"I know I should have told you about Patrick and I'm sorry that I didn't. I know I should have also told you about Becca at the wedding and I'm sorry I didn't do that either. If I had, maybe she wouldn't be in the hospital right now."

Jake stepped onto the deck. "That last part is where you're wrong, Madison. With the problems Becca has, she was bound to get into an accident sooner or later. It's just lucky that no one else got hurt."

"How's she doing?"

"Not great, but she's awake."

"That's a good sign at least. So, she'll be okay?"

Jake shrugged. "She might be if she actually goes to counseling and rehab."

Madison crossed her arms, silently accepting that the old Becca was back. "I'm happy to hear that. You guys will be able to pick up right where you left off." Not waiting for Jake to respond, she walked back to the chair she had been sitting in, picked up her blanket and wine glass and walked inside.

"Whoa, wait, what?" he asked following her.

Madison shrugged her shoulders and kept walking. "Well, Becca's finally doing exactly what you wanted her to, right?"

Jake stepped in front of Madison. "Yeah, but when I was in love with her."

She looked up at him. "You're not in love with her anymore?"

Jake took the blanket and wine glass from Madison's hands and set them on a nearby table. Taking another step closer to her, he brushed the back of his left hand against her cheek. "Of course, I'm not, Madison. I've been in love with you since I opened that stupid door on your face. You're the one I want to be with."

"Why? I feel like I've caused you nothing but grief these last couple of days."

"Yes and no. I wish you had told me about what happened with Becca at the wedding but only because you shouldn't have had to deal with that on your own. I don't know what she said to you but based on things she's said to me I know it couldn't have been nice, so I understand why you didn't say anything. Madison, you're a good person who thinks about other people more than herself and all I can do is think about you. You're passionate, romantic, incredibly smart, beautiful, an excellent golfer, and...we're thinking of going into the same line of work...."

Madison looked at him quizzically.

"I know Evan offered you a second assistant's position at Ruby Lewis after you complete the courses at Guelph."

Madison was taken aback that he knew. Although she had wanted to tell him, any time she tried something had gotten in the way. And despite becoming more open with him about herself she knew that she had not mentioned her golf course management potential. She also remembered asking Evan, her old superintendent, to keep that and her golf course expertise to himself when giving a reference for her at Middleton. She exhaled slowly, "I'm sorry I didn't tell you about that either. I really was going to when we were waiting for Scott's dad to show up with his tow truck and then other things just happened and it just got away from me. I feel like I'm a broken record saying, 'I was going to tell you' and I'm sorry for that. I swear, I don't normally keep secrets."

"Madison, it's okay. With everything that's happened within the last few days and everything before that, I understand why you wouldn't have wanted me or anyone else at Middleton to know. And I believe that you would have told me. Although, I can't say I'm not surprised he wants you in management because you're impeccably talented with every machine and task at the golf course and would make an incredible boss."

Madison blushed. "Thank you. Does anyone else know?"

Jake shook his head. "No, Scott was off talking to other people when Evan mentioned it."

"I'm still not even sure if I'm going to do it-"

"We don't need to talk about it right now," he interrupted her gently. "But I would like to talk about it at some point. And it honestly slipped out of Evan's mouth; we were complimenting your work ethic. He asked me to not say anything, but if we're going to do this." Jake took Madison's hands into his. "And I *want* to do this, I want to start with a clean slate."

Madison did not need to hear any more and threw her arms around his neck, pulling his face to hers. They kissed slowly at first but then passion overtook them, and their kisses became all encompassing. When Madison pulled back, she stared into Jake's eyes and knew she was exactly where she needed to be, where she belonged, and where she was going to stay.

Table of Contents

Chapter One 7
Chapter Two.. 23
Chapter Three.. 35
Chapter Four 49
Chapter Five 57
Chapter Six.. 71
Chapter Seven 83
Chapter Eight 93
Chapter Nine 105
Chapter Ten... 117
Chapter Eleven 143
Chapter Twelve 153
Chapter Thirteen 165
Chapter Fourteen... 173
Chapter Fifteen.. 185

europe books